THE MYSTIC'S TEST

THE MYSTIC'S TEST

Alex Stern

Library of Congress Control Number:		2019903784
ISBN:	Hardcover	978-1-7960-2484-5
	Softcover	978-1-7960-2483-8
	eBook	978-1-7960-2482-1

Print information available on the last page.

Rev. date: 03/28/2019

To order additional copies of this book, contact:
Xlibris
1-888-795-4274
www.Xlibris.com
Orders@Xlibris.com
793783

CONTENTS

To my senior English teacher, Baba, who beat
the grammar rules in my head.

PROLOGUE

In the early afternoon sun, wind howled and gnashed its fangs as it scratched at the stonework of a mystic watchtower. Fortunately, the stone was reinforced with magic, so it didn't move an inch. The only thing that moved were the blue banners inside the tower that depicted the twelve-pointed star with sword handles on the points.

Coming down the stone steps to the sleeping quarters was a man garbed in a gray cloak with a narrowed eye on its back, which was draped over leather armor. His worn face had rough stubble on his chin, and his piercing gray eyes found his five companions resting. Three of them were playing dice, one was asleep, and the other was reading a book.

Sighing for the hundredth time that day, the man entered the sleeping quarters. The room was nondescript, with a few beds and a rack for their weapons. At once, the five occupants, minus the one asleep, jumped to their feet to appear busy.

"Don't bother hiding," the man growled. "I saw you five lounging here, playing dice and reading when you could've been helping to keep this place up to snuff."

The one who had been reading, a woman in her mid-twenties named Sophie, replied, "But, Captain Zanteer, we've cleaned this place within an inch of its life. In fact, what are we even doing here? I want to go back to Minraz."

Zanteer sighed again before fixing on her with his piercing eyes. "As I'm sure you know, we're scouts, which means it's our duty to Minraz to scour Thaysia and make sure we don't have any threats underfoot. Is that unclear?"

Sophie was sweating slightly before shaking her head. With a curt nod, Zanteer walked over to the scout still sleeping. Bending down so his face was next to the scout's ear, he yelled. The scout launched himself into the air and landed sprawling on the floor. His hood slipped, revealing cropped skunk hair and a late teen face. He looked up at the man who had awoken him, and his eyes were stricken with fear.

"Sorry for waking you, Nick, from your pleasant dream. Would you care to tell us about it?"

Nick merely shook his head like a dog ridding itself of flies.

"Good. Now that you're up, you can take watch for the next few hours. What are you waiting for? Get your pockmarked arse up there!" Zanteer barked.

Nick scrambled up the stairs after hastily grabbing his sword. After a minute, the remaining scouts burst out laughing, and even Zanteer's mouth twitched.

Sophie interjected, "Don't you think you were too harsh with the lad? I mean, he only just joined our squad."

Before Zanteer could reply, a scream sliced through the mood. A few seconds later, the tower shook and buckled under the weight of something huge. As the scouts reached out for their weapons, a stream of fire flooded into their room.

Acting quickly, Zanteer raised a barrier of earth in between them and the fire, his face contorted in concentration honed from years of practice as he maintained the earth barrier. After what felt like an eternity, the fire evaporated, leaving Zanteer coated in perspiration. As he gestured to his squad, they barged out the door, only to dive out of the way of another stream of fire.

In front of them was a creature, an elder dragon, that Zanteer had only heard about in stories as a child. It was about a third of the height of the watchtower, with blood-red scales and reptilian yellow eyes that held contempt and hunger. Moving instinctively, the squad scattered as they had been trained. Two of them rushed its flank while summoning spears of water from the stream close by. When the spears made contact, they broke against the scales. Before they could blink, a spiked tail severed two scouts from torso to waist. The air became misted with red, and the blood drove the dragon to continue its killing.

Sophie nodded to her partner, and they combined their respective heat and wind elements. A torrent of superheated air flew at the dragon, but the dragon merely shot its own torrent of fire back. It tore through their attack like it was nothing. They screamed as they were roasted alive.

The smell of cooked human flesh sent nausea through Zanteer as he sent spiked walls of earth at the dragon. The beast merely slashed the walls with its talons, and they crumbled before the dragon severed Zanteer's legs with its tail. With a cry of pain, Zanteer was on his back, with the tail an inch from his skull.

Suddenly, a deep voice stabbed into his mind like a sword of fire— *You fought well, human. However, not well enough*—and the dragon's tail impaled Zanteer's head.

Removing its tail, the elder dragon surveyed the carnage before inhaling deeply. From the corpses, something that resembled compressed air flew into the dragon's nostrils. When all of it was gathered, the dragon crouched down before it shot into the sky.

Flapping its wings, the beast flew toward the volcano on the far east of the land. The dragon didn't arrive until the orb in the sky was intimate with the ground. The earthy ground flew everywhere as the dragon landed outside a large cave, big enough to hold several of his species. Moving forward confidently, the dragon approached a large black orb in the center of the cave.

Given its night vision, the dragon made out the orb perfectly before opening its maw and releasing a stream of compressed fire on the orb. When the fire dimmed, the orb was pulsing rapidly and emitting an eerie orange glow. After a second, a high and commanding voice tore through the dragon's mind.

Very good, my hatchling. I just need another large amount of magic, and I can finally spread my wings and rule this land again. Your next target should be that human settlement—Minraz, I believe it is called. You should gather your strength before you attack and gather the lesser beasts to accompany you.

Dismissed, the elder dragon turned around stiffly and left the cave.

CHAPTER 1

"Nyzir, get your sleeping ass down here, or we're going to miss our graduation!" a feminine voice shouted up the stairs.

Recognizing Sinera's voice, Nyzir began to groggily banish sleep from his citrine eyes. He felt a light yet hard sensation on his nose. Looking down, he saw a purple-and-blue fairy giggling at him. Nyzir swatted the pest away, and the fairy crossed its tiny arms and huffed. Chuckling in wry amusement, Nyzir went to his wash basin and splashed the sleep from his mind.

After combing his short snow-colored hair with agitated finesse, Nyzir went downstairs after putting on a dark purple shirt and pants. When he arrived, his mouth went into ecstasy at the aroma of fresh breakfast. Sitting down at the wooden table, he watched as his sister sat next to him. Sinera looked at her brother with mischievous blue eyes. Her onyx-colored hair cascaded down her head to her shoulders. Her blood-red shirt and dark pants did a good job of hiding her still-developing figure.

Before Nyzir could speak, food arrived, and his fourteen-year-old brain went hazy. His mother had cooked them both chimera eggs and lobster bacon for their graduation from the Mystic Academy.

"I regret to tell you that because of your father's duties with the Forsworn, he won't be home till late tonight," Helena said with sorrow in her hazel eyes, knowing Carter wouldn't be there to see their children become apprentices.

Nyzir and Sinera merely shrugged and ravenously tore into the food with abandon. Then they left the house after giving their mother a hug goodbye.

As the siblings traveled the cobblestone streets, they saw people traveling every which way. They saw civilians rushing to food vendors for house supplies, greeting friends, shopping for clothes and jewelry for either themselves or for their family, and other everyday activities. As they looked around their capital city of Minraz, it still stunned them. From a distance, Minraz could be compared to a multicolored anthill. There was no rule over what color your house or store could be, so the people had definitely taken that to heart. The various houses were every color you could imagine, from bright red to sterling silver, forest green, and even ebony.

The houses inclined steadily before reaching the tallest building in the center, the empress's tower. The tower was coated in white marble that almost blinded anyone who looked at it with the sun behind it. It sent shards of light everywhere as if it were a mirror.

When the siblings reached the Mystic Academy, they gave a nod to the imposing Forsworn that guarded it. Garbed in forest-green tunics over light plate armor, the guards noticed the twelve-pointed star with a sword hilt at each point on their clothing. Nodding back, they allowed them to enter. When they arrived at the classroom, the siblings waited for a few minutes, and then the remaining twenty students arrived, followed by their instructor, Lori. The twenty-five-year-old kept her long auburn hair in a tight ponytail, accompanied with welcoming gray eyes and an athletic figure from her former career as a Forsworn.

As Lori began the lecture before graduation, Nyzir began thinking about what the academy had done for him. After starting out as an awkward ten-year-old, he and the class were given basic training in cardio and endurance, building litheness and muscle mass and learning how to use basic weapons. He at least knew how to swing and block with a sword without losing a limb. Nyzir learned that after training with your master, you had three choices. You could be a Forsworn, the military of Minraz, a mentor, which meant training the next generation of mystics, or a scout, which involved scouring Thaysia for any threats to Minraz.

They were also given a brief introduction to their elemental magic. The four elements were heat, water, earth, and wind, and they each had a sub element—magma for heat, ice for water, crystal for earth—and they all were common to greater and lesser degrees. When asked why wind didn't have a sub element, Lori had smiled sadly and explained that they didn't know. Because magic was passed down genetically, it was encouraged for those with magic to marry and produce offspring as soon as possible.

Empress Sylia was disgusted by this idea and decreed that the age of procreation would be sixteen as the possibility of dying young was still all too common.

"Nyzir, Nyzir, stop daydreaming. It's time for the testing," Sinera hissed in her elder brother's ear, with annoyance oozing out of her lips.

Looking around calmly as if nothing had happened, he noticed Lori calling the students alphabetically. After ten minutes of waiting, Nyzir was called. Sinera gave her brother a reassuring squeeze on the shoulder, and Nyzir left the classroom. As Nyzir traveled down the hall, he saw two male Forsworn guarding the armory door.

"My name's Nyzir. I was called to pick my weapon," Nyzir said, trying to project an aura of nonchalance, but the impassive stares of the guards caused him to shiver.

"Go on in then," the guard on the right side said, and Nyzir entered the armory.

On every wall, there were weapons—swords of all shapes and sizes, one- to two-handed axes, and a couple of hammers. Handling a couple of the swords and axes, Nyzir noticed none fit him. Suddenly, he noticed something gleaming hidden behind some battle-axes. Pulling it out, Nyzir saw it was a halberd. The entire handle was made out of an ebony-colored wood interlaced with metal for protection. The blade was an ax blade that flowed through the wood to a sharp point on the other end. A double-edged dagger blade stuck out the top. The entire weapon was coated with a sheet of dust.

Looking at the other end, Nyzir saw the end of the halberd had a sharpened end for stabbing. However, Nyzir didn't know why this weapon required two stabbing ends. Looking at the middle, he saw a strange grip in the middle of the halberd. Gripping it, Nyzir accidentally twisted it, and suddenly, the halves separated, and he was now holding a pole with the blade and stabbing tip in one hand and a pole with just a stabbing tip in the other. Eyes gleaming with interest, he gave a few experimental swings and found them to feel right in his hands. Reconnecting the halves, he gave the weapon a few twirls and thrusts.

"This is really cool," Nyzir said to himself with glee.

He walked out of the room, and the two guards raised an eyebrow at Nyzir's weapon but didn't comment. Walking down the hall, he reached the elements room. Upon entering, he saw Lori and two other instructors he didn't know. Lori gave her companions a nod, and they pulled out four jars. Each one was filled with its own element.

"Why did you choose that weapon, by the way? It's not common with us," Lori asked.

Nyzir scratched the back of his head and then twirled the halberd. "It feels right to me. Is that a problem?"

No one spoke for a few seconds before Lori cleared her throat and said, "Okay, Nyzir, I want you to close your eyes and concentrate on your element attaching itself to your weapon."

Closing his eyes, Nyzir did as she had asked. A second later, shattering glass was heard, and he felt an odd sensation on both hands. He swore he could hear a pin drop, and he could almost feel their surprise. Opening his eyes, he looked down, and his eyes widened. The top half of the halberd was enclosed with wind swirling around it, while the bottom half was encased in multicolored crystals. What had really shocked him was that at the point where the wind and crystal met, there was no conflict, only a connection in the middle.

Looking back at the instructors, who still needed to recover themselves, he asked uncertainly, "What happens now?"

CHAPTER 2

Lori, always able to regain her composure, said happily, "Well, this is unexpected, I'll tell you that, but I say we save questioning your apparent good fortune for after your celebration with your family." She added a wink. Seeing the confusion on Nyzir's face, she burst out laughing. "Come on, Nyzir. Don't you think your family is going to be so proud when they see their son has a dual affinity fresh out of the academy?"

Still looking pensive, Nyzir said, "My problem isn't with the dual affinities. After all, they're pretty common. My confusion is with how mine are in perfect harmony and almost acting like they're best friends instead of rivals." For emphasis, he showed them where the wind and crystal connected, and he was right. Where there should have been a clash of will, there was only harmony.

"Well, regardless of its weirdness, we will treat this like a blessing and not a curse. Got it, Nyzir?" Lori said this in the mock-serious voice she used only with him. "Though I will say maybe this explains why you always mouth off to me whenever you show up late to class, huh?" she added with a smirk.

"Well, if that's all," Nyzir said with some impatience, "may I go and wait to see how my sister is doing with her testing?"

"Fine. Go already, you ungrateful brat," Lori said in a mock-child voice that she knew infuriated him.

Giving a halfhearted glare to his teacher but a playful smirk, Nyzir returned to the classroom. After waiting for about half an hour, if the clock was anything to go by, Nyzir heard the door open, and before he could blink, his eyes became obscured by a head of black hair. He found himself struggling to not end up on his ass courtesy of his sister's flying hug.

"I passed! What about you? What element do you have? Or did you not pass at all? Tell me, please, Nyzir," Sinera said a little too quickly for Nyzir's brain to catch up.

After removing himself from her death grip, Nyzir replied with his usual slight cockiness, "All right, sis, let's take those one at a time now. First, yes, I did pass. Second, I have a dual affinity. And third, obviously, I passed, or else the previous two points would be negative."

Ignoring her brother's bravado, she instead said, "Anyway, I passed with a dual affinity for water and, bizarrely enough, ice."

The remark that was practically begging to come out, he swallowed back. He decided to question his sister's affinities later and finally got a look at her weapon. It was a standard bow, but what stood out was that instead of wood flowing away from the handle, only the back was wood to hold the string. The front top and bottom of the bow had a single blade that covered the wood perfectly. Both blades connected at the handle to form a seamless blade. On her back, she had a quiver of arrows with raven feathers.

Nyzir said, "Well, that is quite impressive, sis. My weapon is this halberd here." He gestured lazily to it. Then he snatched it up, and before she could react, he twisted the middle and held both ends. "Isn't that something else? Oh yeah, my elements are wind and crystal."

Her reaction was priceless. It was one of the *very* few times he saw his sister dumbstruck. Laughing, he picked up her jaw, and they decided to head home.

On the way home, they made a point of watching the people around them. Most of the civilians smiled and even bowed slightly to the brother-and-sister duo, knowing they had two more protectors. The children laughed and looked at Nyzir and Sinera with admiration. Some of the older mystics gave the two respectful nods and smiles.

When they arrived home, they saw something that nearly gave them a heart attack. They were given a five-star performance of their parents making out at the dining table. Almost in sync, the two teen's faces paled, almost to the color of Nyzir's hair, and then they both made a show of pretending to empty their stomachs on the wood floor. Separating with sheepish looks, Helena and Carter watched the show with amusement.

"Better get used to it, kids. You're going to be doing that in a few years, give or take," Carter said with a wink.

His tanned face was framed by a mop of very dark blue hair. He was muscular with honed reflexes, typical of a Forsworn captain. When questioned about it by their seven-year-old children at dinner, Helena had said, "Oh, don't worry. The curtains match the drapes." She had waited until her husband had taken a sip of blackberry wine, and he nearly died choking.

Now Carter gave his children a hug and eagerly asked, "So what happened? Did you pass?"

Nyzir and Sinera both smiled and pulled out their respective weapons and, as one, summoned their elements. If they had thought the reactions of their teacher priceless, their parents' reactions cranked it up to eleven. After all, it was something to see their on-duty, calm, and collected father with his jaw through the floor. Helena chuckled and picked up her husband's jaw, sealing it with a peck of her lips.   Looking rightfully embarrassed, Carter said, "So, Nyzir, wind and crystal are definitely surprising, but I guess you already want to surpass me, huh, son?" For good measure, he added a ruffle of his son's white hair. "And a halberd, no less. Gee, son, you really are unorthodox. Not a lot of us use those things." Nyzir merely looked sheepish.

Carter continued on to his daughter. "And, Sinera, water and ice do seem to fit you. Maybe this is where you get your bladder control problems from."

Sinera's face put a tomato to shame.

"Aw, come on, sweetie, You need to lighten up every now and again."

Sinera's eyes narrowed before she said, "But, Father, I have to be the sane one of this house to keep you and my dear brother in line."

"Enough, you guys. We should be celebrating, not arguing," Helena said happily.

With that the family left the house to go eat a celebration lunch all the while smiling and laughing.

CHAPTER 3

As the family searched for a good place to eat, Nyzir kept an eye on the populace. The civilians that did notice them smiled, waved, and even did little bows to the family. The rest of them were otherwise busy talking, shopping, or just getting through the day in their own way.

Nyzir had even noticed some mystics around, and when they noticed Nyzir and his family, they too smiled, waved, and even bowed more deeply than the civilians. Hearing an exasperated sigh jerked Nyzir out of his examinations. His father was looking at the people with slight annoyance on his face.

"I still don't get why they bow to us. It's not like we're the empress strolling into town," Carter whispered into his wife's ear.

Helena merely snickered and said slyly, "They bow to you because they know you're powerful, Carter, a Forsworn captain, and as such, dear, you deserve respect."

"You're really not helping me right now, you know, sweetie?" Carter replied with the same sarcasm Nyzir tended to show.

"Oh, I know, dear. Now where should we eat?"

They settled on the Dragon's Bite, a fairly well-known restaurant on the east side of Minraz. The inspiration for the name was quite shocking, to say the least. On the roof of the building, there was a purple dragon head, and in its mouth was half of a chimera. The chimera's snake tail had sunk its fangs into the dragon's clear eye. Thankfully, both had been professionally cleaned before being mounted, and Nyzir really didn't want to know how they cleaned those.

The rest of the two-level building was just as interesting. The outer walls were painted vibrant orange, with white intricate designs inlaid in the wood. On the roof, there were five chimneys for the cooks, and each was a different color. As Nyzir and Sinera opened the ornate doors, the family was greeted by their waitress, who immediately took them to a booth.

Nyzir couldn't help but blush at their waitress, who was a curvy woman and looked to be in her mid-twenties with bright red hair tied in a ponytail. As she stood about half a head taller than Nyzir, it gave him a frontal view of her cleavage, though she apparently didn't mind.

Trying to distract himself, he looked around the restaurant. While not especially big, it did look impressive. There were quite a few ornate lamps hanging from the ceiling, giving the restaurant a pleasant glow. The interior walls were painted ocean blue while interlaced with violet. Everywhere, there were fairies of every color. They were hovering around the occupants, trying to either take snippets of food or just play with a person's hair or clothes. His mother had explained to Nyzir that fairies were tolerated in Minraz because they never attacked humans, so the humans tended to not bother them.

At their booth, Nyzir and his family were given menus and a few minutes to decide. When the waitress returned, Nyzir said, "I think I'll try the phoenix ramen with blueberry wine, please."

"I would like the dragon meat pizza with water to drink," Sinera said with a polite smile.

Then Carter and Helena both ordered a chimera steak with blackberry wine. Giving her charges a warm smile, the waitress left.

"So, kids, what exactly happened at the testing? I have to know," Carter said eagerly.

"I would like to know as well," Helena added.

"All right. I'll go first," Nyzir said. "When I got to the armory, I noticed that none of the weapons fit me, so as I looked around, I found my halberd behind some battle-axes. It just felt right to me, so I took it and went to the testing room. When I got there, Lori told me to concentrate on my element enveloping my weapon. When I did, wind and crystal came on my weapon. Though we were all shocked, Lori told me to be happy, and then I left to wait for Sinera to finish."

Sinera said, "My experience was similar, though I found my bow really quickly. When I arrived at the testing room, I called my element to me, and my bow was covered in water and ice. After congratulating me, Lori bid me farewell."

Their parents looked extremely happy with them, and Carter stood to give them a quick hug before sitting back down just as the food had arrived. As they all dug in, Nyzir noted that the phoenix ramen was indeed very spicy but delicious, especially with the blueberry wine to help. Sinera let him try a bite of her pizza, and it was also delicious, with the dragon meat adding a smoky flavor. When they finished, Carter went to pay, while their waitress helped them clean up.

"Thank you for the truly delicious meal, miss," Nyzir said sincerely. "Oh, don't worry. It was my *pleasure*, dear." As she walked away, she made sure he saw the sway of her hips.

Before Nyzir could do anything, he felt Carter wrap an arm around his shoulders while giving him a smirk. "So my little Nyzir is becoming quite the ladies' man, just like your old man, huh?"

A cough interrupted his teasing, and he saw his wife glaring at him. "I beg your pardon, *dear*. I seem to recall you only having eyes for *me* back in the day, so don't talk about you being a *ladies' man*," Helena added sternly.

"I have to object. After all, I was able to get you to be with me, and you haven't complained once," Carter said indignantly.

"You know," Helena added with her own smirk, "I'm pretty sure I was drunk when you asked me out, and I still don't know what I was thinking."

"Oh, come on. Even Empress Sylia approved of us being together," Carter said.

"That is because she considers you like the son she never had and wanted some grandbabies," Helena added, smiling.

"Hey, don't drag us into this," Nyzir and Sinera said at the same time.

Laughing jovially, Carter and Helena gave each other a small kiss, and the family went back home. When Nyzir got into bed, he thought that today had been one of the best days of his life.

When he awoke, Nyzir tried to remember what was so important about today. Then it hit him. He and Sinera were going to see Empress Sylia about their trial and to meet their new master. Smiling, Nyzir went to pick out some different clothes to celebrate his status as a mystic apprentice. In the end, he settled on gray pants and a dark purple shirt that had the sleeves end at his elbows, and over that, he put on a forest-green trench coat that went down to his knees. For his feet, he chose black boots with metal on the toe ends.

Smiling, Nyzir went downstairs. What he saw slightly shocked him. His mother and father were cooking breakfast, while Sinera sat at the table, waiting patiently. His father was never around in the morning. He took a seat opposite his sister and studied her. She too had a smile on her face and had also changed her wardrobe. Now she wore a white shirt and black pants, and over her shirt, she wore a dark gray cowl.

Before Nyzir could speak, he and Sinera had steaming bowls of oatmeal with fruit in them placed in front of them. Nyzir immediately devoured the food with an abandon that would put a wolf to shame. When they finished, Nyzir and Sinera gave their parents loving hugs and, after grabbing their weapons, left the house.

Nyzir immediately went to an armory shop, with his sister not far behind. When Nyzir reached the counter, he said to the man behind it, "I'm looking for something to hold my halberd. Do you have anything?"
"Of course, young man. Please follow me."

After disappearing for a few minutes, Nyzir returned with a black harness that he had slung across his back. Paying for it with ten gold coins, Nyzir attached his halberd on his back, and then he and Sinera traveled to the empress's tower. When they arrived, a double line of ten Forsworn blocked their path.

Their captain stepped forth. His most distinguishing apparel was the red pauldron he had on his right shoulder. He asked firmly, "What is your business at the empress's tower?"

"We're here to see Empress Sylia about our master, Captain," Nyzir said respectively.

The captain replied, "And what are your names?"

"I'm Nyzir, and this is my sister, Sinera," Nyzir replied smoothly.
"Yes, the empress has been expecting you. May I lead you to her?"

After they had given a nod to the captain, he led the siblings up a flight of stairs before reaching a pair of white double doors with gold writing on them. After the captain knocked three times, a tired "Come in" was heard, and the captain gestured them in.

The throne room was a treat for the eyes. The walls were a pleasant light blue, while the ceiling and floor remained white. On the walls, there were tapestries of both of Sylia's ancestors, famous battles, and even several beasts.

However, it was the empress herself who truly stole the eyes. While she was in her sixties, she still had a more-than-pleasant appearance. She had long silver hair that reached her back, emerald eyes that radiated kindness, and a figure that would make a goddess jealous. When they arrived at her gold-and-silver throne, Nyzir and Sinera immediately got on one knee and bowed to the empress.

"Now how many times have I told you two you shouldn't bow to me?" Empress Sylia said with fatigue in her tone.

"But, Granny Syl, if we didn't, we would be setting a bad example for the rest of the people," Nyzir said teasingly.

Empress Sylia looked miffed and replied, "But we both know I consider you two my grandchildren, and as such, I *order* you two to rise and give me a damn hug."

Laughing, the teens gave their surrogate grandmother the hug, and then she said, "I see you have passed the test. Now your master should be here any time now."

As the words left Sylia's lips, three knocks were heard.

"Come in," Sylia said calmly, and the doors opened.

A young man walked in. He appeared to be in his mid-twenties with messy brown hair. He bore his athletic build with quiet confidence. His clothing was all black and gray, and on his back was a broadsword that looked as long as Nyzir was tall. The pommel of the blade was a griffin's head, and the eyes seemed to glare at Nyzir.

"Ah, Sevastian, it is good to see you again. These two will be your apprentices," Sylia said with a calm smile.

However, before Sevastian could respond, the doors burst open, and a Forsworn ran in.

"There's a griffin attacking the city," the Forsworn said breathlessly. "We need to get you all to safety."

"A griffin? Come on, sis, let's go," Nyzir said, grabbing his sister's hand and leading her out of the tower.

A chuckle was heard from Sevastian, who said, "Well, I better go too. After all, if they're to be my apprentices, I need to see them in action firsthand." Then he left at a run.

When Nyzir and Sinera left the tower, they saw a mob of people running for their lives. A screech was heard in the sky, and Nyzir saw the griffin get its right wing badly burned, courtesy of heat magic, and it went crashing down. The street shook from the impact.

Nyzir immediately began pushing his way through the crowd to get at the griffin. When he arrived, he saw the griffin up close for the first time. It was as large as a one-story house with a white feathered chest and brown feathers on its back and rear end. The beak was bronze and looked as long as Nyzir's forearm. Its wings were in bad shape. One appeared to have been crushed on impact with the ground, while the other was black with red flecks still on it.

Nyzir pushed his way through as the Forsworn surrounded the beast. He drew his halberd. He was about to be grabbed when a voice said, "Don't. I want to see how my newest apprentice will handle this." Sevastian had appeared and spoken loudly enough for them all to hear.

Nyzir saved his focus for the beast before him. He saw that its golden eyes were filled with the hatred of seeing a mortal enemy. It gave a shriek at Nyzir, who flinched but otherwise kept his cool. The griffin slowly advanced and then leapt with claws outstretched for Nyzir. Acting on instinct, Nyzir rolled in between the claws, and as he found himself face to belly with the griffin, he thrust his halberd into the beast's feathery stomach and dragged it along the griffin's body until it came free at the back end.

The griffin collapsed with blood pooling around it from the long deep gash in its body. Nyzir got to his feet, and disconnecting the halberd, he hurled the bottom end into the griffin's neck. Even as the sharpened end pierced its feathery neck, the griffin began thrashing around, trying to hit Nyzir with its tail.

Jumping back, Nyzir thought of something, pointing the top half of his halberd at the griffin. He envisioned a crystal shooting through the griffin's head. Nyzir felt a cool sensation come through his body and channel through the halberd and settle into the ground. Then with a sound like breaking glass, a large multicolored crystal rose fast from the ground and impaled the griffin's head. It still had that look of hatred as its now lifeless eyes stared at Nyzir.

Shaking slightly, Nyzir approached the griffin's corpse. After pulling out the other half of his halberd and reconnecting the halves, he bent down and pulled out a bunch of feathers and cut off some talons. As he started to walk, his legs gave out, and he supported himself on his halberd as Sinera rushed to her brother's side. Grabbing a hold of Nyzir's other arm, she led him out of the crowd. Before they got out, Nyzir saw Sevastian give him a proud smile and a wink.

CHAPTER 4

While Nyzir slept to recover from his battle, far to the east, in a dense forest, a group of hunters were stalking the forest in search of a meal. They were five in number. The full moon revealed each to have a hooked nose and twisted mouth that gave the appearance of a permanent sneer.

After thirty minutes of not finding anything, the family of hunters was getting frustrated. One of the sons decided to take his frustration out on a green snake that was under a bush. While the others were talking about what they would do next, the young man went to step on the snake. Just before the boot landed, the snake struck, wrapping itself around his leg and sinking its fangs into the man's calf, and dragged him into the bushes.

The other four men wheeled around as they heard a pair of jaws snapping up flesh, meat, and bone coupled with an ear-piercing scream. Becoming scared, the four remaining hunters made a mad dash for their village. Before they got very far, they saw the same snake hanging from a tree branch. The snake seemed to have a predatory smile on its lips as it eyed the hunters.

Then one hunter made the mistake of looking at something else, and the reptile struck. Paralyzing venomous fangs sunk into shoulder flesh as the snake flung the body into the forest. After a minute of silence, once again, there was the sound of tearing flesh. The three remaining hunters were now shaking in fear as they made a mad run for the village gate while having a horrible thought that they, the hunters, were now being hunted.

They didn't get far when the snake struck, striking one of the older men and then moving onto the second oldest, sticking its fangs into the man's neck, and hurled him away while leaving the other one on the dirt. The last young man was now beyond terrified. His brothers, father, and uncle had been killed, and he didn't even know what was doing it. No snake was that strong.

Before he could run, the snake bit him on the leg and hurled him against a tree. As he was paralyzed, he couldn't turn his head, but he could move his eyes, so he strained to see what was happening. Then across from him in the shelter of trees, something big was moving toward him.

In the darkness, he saw was a vague shape slowly moving toward him. All he could see in the darkness were three pairs of blood-red eyes staring solely at him. Just as the creature pounced, a sliver of moonlight illuminated a tiny bit of the creature. All the young man saw was two different colors of fur, golden brown and gray, streaked with blood and organs. A moment later, a large mouth full of red-colored teeth sent him to blackness.

Nyzir, Sinera, and Sevastian stood before Empress Sylia in her throne room a few days after the attack. As opposed to the kind, grandmotherly visage Sylia usually showed when in the presence of Nyzir and Sinera, her emerald eyes held a serious look that they rarely saw.

"The reason I have called you three here is for a number of things. I want to know what you think of your potential apprentices, Sevastian, and I want to hear from Nyzir about his battle with the griffin as it pertains to what I must tell you," Sylia said while flicking her eyes to each person in tow.

Sevastian, knowing honesty was what would help him, said, "Well, the boy definitely has the skill to be able to take down a flightless griffin singlehandedly, and the way he employed both the unique function of his weapon and his element speaks to his tactical awareness. Now as to if I will train them, I have not seen his sister's skill with her bow or her element, so she will be a little tricky, but I will consent to giving these two a chance if they can prove to me they are worthy."

"That is an excellent summary, Sevastian, which is why I assigned you these two. You have the knowledge to train them in both their weapon and their elements, and you have the ability to not smother the hard truth with comforting lies," Sylia said with a smile before pulling out a note from her robe. "I received this note from a messenger bird yesterday, which is why I called you here. It tells of an attack on a family of hunters two nights ago. The bodies were all torn up and were scattered around. The only evidence seen was some large paw prints in the dirt as well as what appeared to be snake bites in all the victims. As I don't have the knowledge of every creature on our continent of Thaysia, I'll differ to you, Sevastian."

"From what I've read and seen, all the markings point to a chimera as the snake bites would be from its snake tail, and the torn-up carcasses would likely be from the feline main body. It would also explain the large footprints as a chimera is about as big as the griffin that Nyzir faced. As to the attack happening at night, normally, chimeras aren't nocturnal hunters, and they prefer to attack at first opportunity. If the bodies were thrown around, it would suggest the snake's work, but I've never heard of a chimera doing such things. Usually, it would just charge in and kill anyone it deemed prey, but this one seemed to let the snake handle the work while also instilling fear into its prey. Honestly, I don't know what to make of this."

Nyzir, deciding to speak then, said, "I noticed when I fought the griffin that it looked at me with an unusual amount of hatred. Not hunter-and-prey dynamic but the sort of hatred you show to someone you hate with every fiber of your being. Something was definitely wrong with the griffin, but I don't know what."

Sylia replied, "All right, Sevastian. I believe Nyzir's story. As a request, while you're training them, could you please keep an eye out for any more strange behaviors from these creatures?"

"I'll be sure to keep an eye on any beasts I see," Sevastian consented, "but I'm not sure what we can gain from it."

"Very well then. You are all dismissed to pack up and get out of Minraz for your training," Sylia said smoothly.

However, before they could leave, the doors opened, and the Forsworn captain of her tower came in and said, "High Empress, we require you in the interrogation room. We have captured a goblin snooping around Minraz, and it appears he has some information on that griffin attack."

"Nyzir, Sinera, and you, Sevastian, accompany me. I want you to hear this as well," Sylia said imperiously as the group traveled to the interrogation chamber under the empress's tower.

Upon their arrival, the guards allowed them entrance. The interrogation room was a small room lit only by a single oil lamp hanging from the ceiling. In the middle of the room, strapped to a table, was the goblin. He was rather short, coming up only to Nyzir's stomach. His skin was blood red, with pointed ears, sharp pointed teeth, and black eyes that had that same unusual hatred in them.

"I was told you may have some information on why we were attacked a couple of days ago by a griffin. Can you enlighten us?" Sylia said.

"I don't know nor give a mug of your human crap why a griffin would attack you," the goblin replied in a guttural voice.

Nyzir said, "Sylia, may I try something on our little friend here? I might be able to get him to talk."

Sylia was clearly deep in thought when she said, "Very well, but don't go overboard."

Nyzir nodded and grabbed his halberd and pointed it at the goblin's head. He imagined the air around the goblin's head was slowly being drawn into the tip of his weapon. While it didn't look like anything was happening, the goblin began to thrash, and his eyes bugged out as he tried to inhale, only to find nothing. Just as his skin was beginning to pale, Nyzir released the air. The goblin began hacking and inhaling great amounts of air before collapsing back on the table.

In a shaky voice, the goblin said, "You think you're safe behind these walls and behind your pitiful magic. My master will have his revenge for what you did to him."

Sylia spoke then. "What master, and what have we done to him to warrant these attacks?"

The goblin chuckled throatily and said, "You are not worthy of his name, but know this. You human swine may have defeated him, but he is not dead, and soon, he will have his revenge on all you magic-wielding abominations." The goblin lay back down and said no more.

Sylia said, "Sevastian, because of this information, it is paramount that you train these two as much as you can so that when we are attacked, we will be ready to kill this threat."

"I understand, Empress, and I will make sure these two are the strongest I can make them by the time this master makes his move. Come on, you two. We need to leave and get you two up to snuff. Go pack what you need and meet me at the stables in an hour."

The siblings immediately bolted for their house.

CHAPTER 5

Upon entering their house, Nyzir and Sinera went to their rooms and began packing food, extra clothes, and other essentials. Nyzir grabbed a single-edged white dagger that he had had made from the griffin talon and slid it in his belt. Sunlight streamed through the window of his room, which made the brown and white feathers that decorated his halberd glow.

Arriving in the kitchen, Nyzir saw Sinera hugging their parents. On her hip was an identical dagger that Nyzirhad given her from the second griffin talon. After giving Carter and Helena their hug, Nyzir practically dragged his sister to the stables.

Nyzir, with Sinera in tow, dashed through the marketplace that separated the mystic living quarters from Minraz's outer gates. They swerved and navigated through the bustle with some difficulty. The populace either got out of the way unharmed or was unintentionally shoved out of the way, with their response being a stinging glare.

When they arrived, they found Sevastian, but he wasn't alone. Lori was standing in front of him, talking urgently. After a few seconds, she gave Sevastian a swift but hard kiss on the lips before running back to the academy. Nyzir then noticed three saddled unicorns, presumably their mounts. The unicorns were different colors of white, storm gray, and brown. The only common factor was the star-white horn just above their eyes. Mounting the unicorns, the master and students galloped out of Minraz.

After riding for a day, they stopped in a grotto to rest. After dismounting, Nyzir and Sinera went to tether the unicorns, while Sevastian went to gather firewood and dinner. When Sevastian returned with a family of dead rabbits and a couple of twigs, he immediately went to work on making roasted rabbit with his heat element.

While the food cooked, Sevastian said, "Nyzir, I have to request that you never use your magic the way you used it on that goblin again. Magic is not a tool to be used whenever you feel like it. Instead, you should use it if you have no other option because of the demands of magic. The reason you were limping after your fight with the griffin was because your body was not used to using that much magic, and thus, you could barely walk."

"Isn't there a way to train your body so it can take the strain of the magic?" Nyzir asked.

"That could be done with a combination of experimenting with your magic and endurance training, but even that can only help so much."

Suddenly, there was the sound of snapping wood, and instantly, Sevastian was on his feet, with his broadsword in hand. After a few seconds, Sevastian gestured for Nyzir and Sinera to grab their weapons just as five men in brown-and-green garb with plated chest armor ran at them. Immediately, the leader made a beeline for Sevastian, while his companions attacked Nyzir and Sinera in pairs, separating them.

Nyzir went on the defensive, using his halberd to both block and deflect the bandit's wild sword attacks. Realizing he couldn't keep this up for long, Nyzir decided to try wind magic. Separating from his assailants, Nyzir made a gust of wind blow the bandits back across the grotto. Taking advantage of this, Nyzir ran to his downed foes and quickly killed both with a thrust through the heart and neck. Blood flew in arcs from where the wounds were, and some splattered on Nyzir's face. He froze, feeling the sticky substance on his face, seeing the men he had killed looking at him with lifeless eyes. Taking a deep breath, he wiped the blood off.

Looking toward his sister, he saw that she had already killed one of her enemies with a slash across the chest, while the other one was pressing the attack, attempting to simply power through her defense. Suddenly, he stumbled on a tree root, and Sinera, not wasting a moment, took her enemy's head off with a precise swipe of her bladed bow.

Hearing a grunt of pain had them whirl around to find Sevastian holding his arm as there appeared to be spikes made of earth in his arm. The bandit attempted to hack him with his ax, but Sevastian parried the strike with his broadsword and then grabbed the man by his shirt. His hand grew red hot, and after a second, there was the smell of cooking meat. The bandit leader's body began to glow red for a few seconds and then stopped, and the bandit's body went limp.

Nyzir suddenly said, "How could a bandit use earth magic like that? I thought only we could use magic."

Sevastian replied, "That would be because he was one of us, but he is now a Forsaken, meaning he cut all ties with Minraz and betrayed our trust. Bastards, the lot of them!" He spat on the corpse and had a look of disgust in his eyes.

As Nyzir looked at the corpses and saw the red-turned-brown blood splotched on green and brown soil, bile rose in his throat, and he ran to a bush and retched out yesterday's food. With a look of revulsion, Nyzir grabbed a wineskin and wet his throat with the soothing liquid. Still shaking, Nyzir sat down with his sister, who looked similarly queasy but held it in as Sevastian served the rabbit.

Sevastian said, "I understand your first kill can affect you negatively. However, the way I get through it is to ask myself, 'What would have happened if I had let him kill me?'"

"They would have no doubt killed you, Sevastian, and me and then most likely take Sinera for either slavery or even just use her for their pleasure," Nyzir said, clenching his fists while hate blazed in his citrine eyes.

Sinera looked shocked, but then her eyes hardened, and she gripped her bow tighter. "I wouldn't have let them have their way with me. I would have found a way to stop them," Sinera said with conviction, but there was fear in her blue eyes.

Nyzir wrapped an arm around his sister's shoulder and squeezed her gently. In response, she leaned into him with a contented smile on her face.

Sevastian smirked and said, "So what else is going on between you two?"

Nyzir and Sinera jumped apart with blushes on their faces.

"Relax. I know nothing's going on, and even if it were, I wouldn't care. Didn't the instructors teach you that because of your magic, you can have a relationship with each other if wanted? It's just not encouraged."

Nyzir and Sinera turned the shade of a tomato.

Sevastian almost landed in the fire from laughing so hard. "Anyway, the fact that you two acknowledge this is proof that you have grown a little more. Remember to use your magic not as a tool but as a shield to protect your family and a sword to strike out at those who would see harm to your loved ones."

With that said, Sevastian absorbed the fire into his sword and went to sleep on his blanket. With blushes still present and not daring to look at each other, Nyzir and Sinera followed suit.

CHAPTER 6

Nyzir felt he had slept only five minutes when something cold and wet shattered his waking dreams like a pane of glass. Coughing and choking, Nyzir sat up and saw Sevastian standing over him with an empty bucket.

"Good, you're up now. Grab your weapon while I wake your sister," Sevastian said it as if this was normal for him.

The sky was still dark, and only the barest streaks of pink on the horizon told Nyzir the sun would rise in a few hours. Grasping his halberd, Nyzir heard a shriek of surprise as, sure enough, Sinera woke while sputtering.

"Now as you two are awake, I will tell you how your schedule will be for now. I will train you in melee combat in the mornings and magic in the afternoons. However, Sinera, because you have ice as well as water, I will be taking you to the northern tribes to see if they will train you as I don't know the fundamentals of ice manipulation." After taking a breath, Sevastian continued, "You two will spar with each other until I say stop so I can evaluate your skill with your weapons."

"Uh, Master, what if we get wounded while we spar with our weapons? They're not blunted," Nyzir said, looking concerned while Sinera nodded.

Sevastian's eyes took on a gleam, and a moment later, a sadistic grin swept over his features, and he slowly raised his right arm. His hand began to turn red before brightening to the point where it illuminated his face and the green foliage around them.

"Don't worry, kiddies. If need be, I could always cauterize the wound for you," he said, with that grin threatening to split his face.

By now, Nyzir and Sinera were sweating bullets from their master's expression, and they were shaking like leaves blowing in a breeze.

"Th-that won't be necessary, Sevastian. It was just a slip of the tongue," Nyzir responded quickly.

In an instant, the visage of sadism washed away from Sevastian, and he said happily, "Good. Now you two take positions opposite each other, and when I give the signal, you two fight with weapons only, no magic."

Nyzir and Sinera stood opposite each other, weapons in hand, when Sevastian shot a spark of heat into the air, and the two combatants began circling. Nyzir studied his sister for anything he could use to his advantage. All he got was a twitch of Sinera's lips before she leapt at him while swiping her bow in a wild rush. Holding his ground, Nyzir spun his halberd and frantically deflected her strikes. Sinera launched a roundhouse kick that Nyzir intercepted with his halberd while countering with a punch to his sister's gut.

Sinera rolled with the punch before attacking Nyzir again. He retreated slowly under his sister's onslaught and searched his surroundings for an advantage when he saw to his far right a clump of dirt. Gaining an idea, Nyzir slowly retreated to the right, while Sinera kept up the pressure. Arriving at his destination, Nyzir spun his halberd and whacked the clump of dirt into Sinera's face. With a cry of shock and pain, Sinera stumbled back while frantically trying to get the dirt clear. Acting quickly, Nyzir swept Sinera's feet out from under her with his halberd. Before she could recover, Sinera found Nyzir's halberd at her throat. Before she could say anything, the sound of clapping was heard. Looking over, Nyzir and Sinera saw Sevastian clapping with a smile on his face.

"That was very good, you two. I now know where your strengths and weaknesses lie in melee combat. Nyzir, that was, dare I say it, brilliant, with using the dirt to end the fight. At the same time, you won't always have those options in battle, so you need to work on actually fighting back. Sinera, your offense was good, but it left you open to Nyzir's counter. You must balance out offence and defense. Is that understood?"

"Yes, Master," Nyzir and Sinera said at the same time.

"Now then, I want you two to go up against me, and you can use both magic and weapon if you so desire. Now get on your feet and get ready."

Nyzir helped his sister up, and she gave him a grateful smile before whispering in his ear. A predatory smile found its way to Nyzir's face, and he nodded before both got ready.

Sevastian drew his broadsword and made a "come here" motion with his hand. Not rising to the bait, Nyzir gripped his halberd and began to circle Sevastian. The instant her master's attention was distracted, Sinera knocked an arrow and released it with a *twang*, and the arrow flew toward Sevastian's chest. With reflexes honed only through rigorous training, Sevastian deflected the arrow. The moment he did, Nyzir struck.

Nyzir launched an offensive barrage of strikes interlaced with punches and kicks that, no matter how wildly he alternated, Sevastian always intercepted either with his broadsword or with his own arms and legs. Getting desperate, Nyzir attempted to stagger his master by hitting him hard in the leg. However, before it made contact, Sevastian jumped and, using the halberd as a springboard, launched himself at Sinera. She attempted to slice him with her bow, but he did a forward roll and, in the process, grabbed her leg and forced her to a new level of intimacy with the ground. Finishing the roll, Sevastian kept his distance as Nyzir rushed to his sister's aid.

Helping Sinera to her feet, Nyzir whispered quickly in Sinera's ear. Nodding back, Sinera grabbed her bow as she and Nyzir attacked Sevastian. Rushing him from both the right and left, the siblings attacked simultaneously at his chest and legs. Moving as fluidly as water, Sevastian pivoted backward and let his students' weapons clash before tripping them both with a leg sweep.

However, an instant later, they were back on their feet again, attacking together. Making a mental note on their teamwork skill, Sevastian continued to dance his way around their attacks and kept them stumbling into each other. Getting frustrated, Nyzir and Sinera attacked with everything they had. All it got them was a powerful sidekick to Sinera's abdomen that threw her to the other side of the grotto while Sevastian twisted Nyzir's wrist and threw his halberd to the side.

Sevastian thrust his broadsword at Nyzir, while his student put his arms in front of him in a desperate X block. Closing his eyes, Nyzir waited for the pain of being stabbed, but nothing happened. All he heard was the sound of metal striking something hard. As he opened his eyes, Nyzir's jaw threatened to leave his face. Nyzir's arms appeared to be encased in gauntlets made of crystal. The broadsword hadn't even pierced the crystal.

Recovering from his shock, Nyzir saw a similar look of shock and even satisfaction on his master's face before Nyzir grabbed the broadsword with his hand and threw it away. Moving quickly, Nyzir punched Sevastian in the abdomen with all the strength he could muster, which caused Sevastian to go flying before landing on his back. Looking at his sister, Nyzir saw the look of shock on Sinera's face before she rose to her feet gingerly while clutching her stomach before giving Nyzir a hug. Then the two both helped Sevastian to his feet.

Looking at his students, Sevastian smiled and said, "Well done, you two. After I've recovered, we'll move on to your next stage of training."

It turned out that Sevastian's recovery involved drinking from his wineskin and having some of the leftover rabbit he had hunted last night. After his meal, he began searching for the bandits who had attacked them. With a smirk, he tossed Nyzir and Sinera several pouches. When they opened them, they revealed quite a bit of gold.

"I have more than enough gold for myself, so you two can keep it. I get the feeling it will come in handy," Sevastian said.

After that, Sevastian took the siblings on an hour-long walk through the woods before reaching a cliff face.

Sevastian said, "Now, Nyzir, you discovered one of the properties of your magic, the ability to use crystal as armor. Now I will teach you how to use your wind magic to fly."

Nyzir's eyes gleamed, and he looked excited at the prospect.

"Now to fly, you must concentrate on the wind currents lifting you and then guide yourself to where you want to go."

With that said, Sevastian picked up Nyzir and, ignoring his surprised yelp, threw him off the cliff. Sinera cried out in shock and made a dash for her brother before Sevastian grabbed her by the scruff of her neck.

"Don't worry, my dear. He will be just fine . . . I hope."

Nyzir was doing what anyone in his position would do—screaming. Desperately contorting himself, he could see he was falling very quickly. He racked his brain to think of what to do. Remembering what Sevastian had said, he gripped his halberd and called the wind to stop his descent.

The winds seemed to envelope him and caress him as a lover would. For an instant, he felt at peace with the soothing wind in his ears and the feeling of weightlessness that made him feel like he was underwater. Then the currents of air shot him into the sky per his request, and soon, he was spinning in the air, doing somersaults, twists, and whatever he could think of before noticing Sevastian and Sinera watching him with satisfaction and awe on their faces.

It was at this point that the wind slipped away with something akin to a laugh before Nyzir dropped. Thinking fast, Nyzir called the wind to slow his descent. Though it did so, he still had to turn his landing into a roll to avoid injury. Nyzir saw Sinera and Sevastian run over to him and embrace him in a group hug.

"Nyzir, my boy, I knew you could do it. Good use of quick thinking, and it just appears you need to be able to maintain flight as you now know how to do it. Uh, why are you looking at me like that?"

Nyzir had a hard and angry look in his citrine eyes before giving a solid kick to his master's lower region. Reacting casually, Sevastian dodged to the right, and Nyzir lost his balance and landed on his side.

"Now, kid, that was very rude, you know. I understand how you feel, but that doesn't justify kicking me in my jewels. Besides, I have a girlfriend back home who would very much appreciate future children, thank you," Sevastian said snidely.

Glaring, Nyzir gestured to return to their camp. When they arrived, Nyzir sat down, while Sinera and Sevastian sat opposite him and waited patiently for him to speak.

"I have to say, Master, even though you could have killed me, that was exhilarating, to say the least," Nyzir said.

"Well, I'm glad you at least had fun, Nyzir. I'll be sure to not make it so easy next time," Sevastian said with that same smile he had shown earlier.

Suppressing a shudder, Nyzir glanced around their camp. Lying on the ground, partially concealed by bushes, a green snake watched the trio. Nyzir noticed the stare and noted the large amount of foliage where the snake was. He even thought he had seen something shift slightly behind the bushes and trees.

Sevastian, in his best lecture voice, intoned, "Just so you know, Sinera, the dirt we're on also contains moisture, so if you want, you could use the water from the ground in a fight if need be."

"I'll be sure to remember that, Master," she said with a smirk that looked like her brother's.

Nyzir locked eyes with Sevastian and discreetly gestured to his left. Looking peripherally, Sevastian noticed the snake's stare.

His eye narrowed slightly before he said, "Well, Nyzir, I must say your magic skill is impressive. We just need to work on your variety of skills." Nudging Sinera, Sevastian flicked his eyes to the snake, and she followed his gaze.

Sinera slightly tensed but relaxed an instant later. She said, "Yeah, Nyzir, you're showing impressive magic ability, but don't get cocky. Soon, I'll be moping the floor with your hide."

Laughing, Nyzir slowly drew his halberd. The snake seemed to tense up until Nyzir brought out a stone and made a show of polishing the blade. The snake relaxed slightly, and Nyzir took his opening. He gripped his halberd tighter while sending crystal magic through the earth and detected something large. Smiling wickedly, Nyzir summoned several large spikes of crystal.

A roar shook the air and made the ground tremble as the chimera broke the crystals and lunged at its prey. Immediately, the three scattered, with the chimera swiping at them with claws and tail. The chimera looked like a childhood nightmare come alive, with the feline head snarling, with bloodied fangs showing. The goat on its back looked at the three with contempt in its red eyes, while the snake tail swayed while eyeing them almost coyly. The horror was highlighted by the large crystals sticking out of its body, with black blood dripping on the dirt. The hungry gleam in its ruby eyes told Nyzir that it found them appetizing.

Jumping back, Nyzir inhaled a mouthful of air before spitting out balls of compressed air that looked like they hurt like hell when hitting the chimera's hide and opening fresh wounds. The beast gave another ear-splitting roar before striking Nyzir with its paw, which sent him flying. Sevastian, with broadsword in hand, rushed the chimera's flank and, while dodging the tail, sliced off the snake in a spray of blood. Screaming in pain, the chimera attempted a back kick, but Sevastian's dive rolled him out of reach. Sinera jumped using a fallen tree as a springboard. She launched herself over the chimera while firing arrow upon arrow. The chimera howled in pain and seemed to redouble its efforts to eat them. Nyzir shakily rose to his feet and, gathering his magic, pointed his halberd at the chimera and made a circling motion. After a second, a mini cyclone shot out of the halberd and struck the chimera in the side, blasting the beast into a couple of trees.

After a few seconds, the chimera leapt back into the fray, its right side looking partially shredded from the cyclone. The beast seemed to be drawing on the pain to continue the fight, which would explain its tenacity. The goat on its back sent a stream of pure magic energy that forced the trio to scatter from the blast. The chimera swiped at Sevastian, which he easily dodged, but the remainder of the tail lashed out and struck

Sevastian with the strength of a sledgehammer. Crashing into some trees, a dazed Sevastian only saw the lunging monster and braced himself for the darkness.

Suddenly, a dome of crystal surrounded him, and the chimera's claws only scratched the surface before it retreated to avoid a barrage of air bullets. The dome shattered, and Sevastian saw Nyzir and Sinera in front of him. Both looked bloody and bruised, with Nyzir looking exhausted but determined despite large claw marks on his chest. Sinera looked like she had been thrown around violently, with bruises and cuts on her face.

"What are you guys doing? You two need to get out of here!" Sevastian cried out desperately.

"But, Master, you said we should use our magic to protect our friends and family," Nyzir said sharply.

"And last I checked, Master, you qualify," Sinera said while readying herself.

Tears started to leak from Sevastian's eyes as he saw his pupils ready to die for him. Sinera closed her eyes, and suddenly, a large blast of water shot out of the ground and struck the chimera in the face and blinded the creature.

Sevastian shakily rose to his feet and said, "Nyzir, can you manage one more of those cyclones of yours?"

"I should be able to, but why?"

"Just trust me, Nyzir. Do it *now!*"

Nyzir summoned a mini cyclone. As it was formed, he saw Sevastian infusing it with waves of heat. By now, an incredibly hot cyclone engulfed the chimera in a blaze of yellow and orange that illuminated the surrounding forest. When it died, all that was left was a smoking, burnt, and dead chimera.

Suddenly, blackness closed on Nyzir, and the last thing he saw was Sinera catching him before he hit the ground.

CHAPTER 7

The first thing Nyzir noticed before opening his eyes was that he was lying on something soft. Opening his eyes, he blinked at the oil lamp on a table next to him. He was lying on a comfy bed. The room was bare of decoration save for a single window. The wood door opened, and a woman entered. Judging by the state of her dirty and torn brown dress and the sorrow in her eyes, she was not treated well.

"Good morning, sir. Your friends are eating right now if you want to join them," she said.

Nyzir slowly got out of bed before putting a hand on the wall for support as slight nausea came over him. Swallowing back the disgusting bile, he noticed his wounds seemed to be gone. "What happened to me? I thought I was wounded," Nyzir said.

"Well, the girl you're with did something with water, and your body healed all those nasty wounds," she said with intrigue in her eyes.

"Really? I'll have to talk to her about that," Nyzir said groggily before again noticing her state of apparent mistreatment.

Getting an idea, Nyzir opened the window and peered at the soil. He began summoning crystals to the surface. It took a second. Then multicolored crystals sprouted out of the ground before taking the shape of a rose in bloom. With a satisfied smile, Nyzir turned back to the woman and handed her the rose. Shakily, she took the rose and held it like a newborn babe.

"Take this and use it to get yourself some new clothes and try to find another form of employment," Nyzir said sincerely.

Tears streamed down her face. She gently put the rose on the bed before tackling Nyzir in a flying hug. "Thank you, thank you. I will never forget this." For added measure, she gave him a chaste kiss on the cheek before untangling herself from Nyzir. A blush crossed her face. She then left quickly after grabbing the rose and tucking it away.

Smiling, Nyzir left the room. Looking around the tavern, Nyzir spotted Sinera and Sevastian sitting at a table. He plopped down opposite them with a smile before pulling a bowl of fruit porridge to himself and ravenously devoured the food. Sinera and Sevastian raised a brow but otherwise waited.

Pushing the empty bowl away, Nyzir said, "So where are we? What happened? And what's next for us?"

Sevastian replied, "We are about half a mile from a series of underground tunnels, which will be your next phase of training. You've been sleeping for three days, which explains your hunger."

Nyzir's eyes widened in shock, and he almost choked from gasping before managing to get down his food. Nyzir asked shakily, "Oh yeah, sis, I wanted to ask. What happened to my injuries?"

Sinera blushed slightly before saying, "I was able to heal you with my water element. Was it not satisfying, Nyzir?"

"No, no, it was excellent. I'm feeling much better except for this fatigue," he replied.

Sevastian, deciding to speak, said, "Well, kiddo, with what you did a few days ago, I'd be exhausted to."

There was something different about him. His eyes held a new light of genuine happiness as opposed to teasing. The way he spoke to them reminded Nyzir of the times his mother would read Sinera and him stories as little kids. Smiling, Nyzir said, "I wonder, Master, could I possibly try trading the crystals I make for money?"

"What brought this up, Nyzir?" Sevastian replied.

"I gave a crystal rose to that woman who visited me and told her to try and use it to live a better life. I wanted to know if I could use them for getting us money if we need it," Nyzir said eagerly.

For a second, Sinera had a look of jealousy in her blue eyes before she smoothed her facial expression quickly.

"I don't see any fault in the idea, Nyzir, but let's save that for later. You two will have a hard day ahead of you."

With that said, Sevastian stood and beckoned his students to follow. With a shrug, they left the tavern and were temporarily blinded by the new dawn. The small town itself wasn't much to look at. Most of the houses were made of tree logs, while the roofs were made out of either woven plant life or rotten wood. Opposite the tavern was a blacksmith shop, and down the road, there were several small homes. They found their mounts just outside town, tethered to a post for horses. The unicorns gazed at the trio with intelligent eyes before Nyzir's gave him a slobbery lick on his cheek.

"Yeah, I missed you too, my friends," Nyzir said soothingly while stroking the unicorn's gray hide.

Mounting, Sevastian led them half a mile out of the village before they came across a series of tunnel entrances embedded into the side of a small mountain that cast them in pleasant shadow.

When they reached the tunnels, Sevastian said, "This is the next part of your training, you two. I was looking at these entrances while you were taking your nap, Nyzir, and I think these tunnels aren't natural. Someone or something dug them."

Nyzir and Sinera looked confused as to the point.

"Your goal today is to both try to find out what created these tunnels and survive down there for a day," he said nonchalantly with a pinch of seriousness.

"What if we get lost down there? We don't know how deep these tunnels go," Nyzir said, looking uncertain.

Sevastian sighed and put a hand on both Nyzir and Sinera's shoulders. "All right, listen, you two. This is to show me that you two can survive down there without me, even if it's just for a day. I won't be able to protect you from everything out there, though I wish I could, believe me. You need to be able to trust in each other and know you have each other's back."

As he said this, Nyzir saw a flash of pain in Sevastian's eyes before they lit up with mirth.

"Besides, I took a leap of faith with young Nyzir here, and he proved to me he can adapt. Now I want to learn if you two can put your life in each other's hands," After a pause, he said, "What are you waiting for? Get your asses down there and show me why you two are worthy of learning from me."

With a yelp, Nyzir and Sineraran into the tunnels. After running through the tunnels for a few minutes, navigating twists and turns, they stopped, panting before looking around. The darkness weighed on them like a thick blanket that was quickly becoming suffocating. Thinking quickly, Nyzir summoned two small crystals out of the side of the tunnel. Picking them up, Nyzir gazed at them quizzically. As he pumped some more magic into the crystal, a grin split his face as the crystals let out a multicolored glow. It was as if the tunnel was encased in a rainbow. Handing one to Sinera, Nyzir led the way down the tunnel. The lights illuminated the hard rock and gave it an ethereal glow. After a minute of walking in silence, they found multiple other tunnels branching out from theirs.

"Do you think we should split up and cover more ground?" Sinera asked.

"Didn't you listen to those stories Mom used to tell us?" Nyzir replied quickly. "We never split up unless we want to die."

That shut her up. Nyzir and Sinera took the far right tunnel but not before Nyzir planted a crystal in the shape of an arrow into the cave wall, pointing the way they had come.

They continued deeper into the network of tunnels. Normally, they weren't claustrophobic, but the tunnels seemed to be trying their damnedest to beat it into them. Every now and then, they would come upon another series of tunnels to choose from. Every time, Nyzir would insert a crystal arrow pointing the way back. It was impossible to know how long they were down there—ten minutes, an hour, two hours. Coupled with the fact that all the tunnels looked identical to one another, it felt like they were walking in circles.

The smell of burned and charred meat assailed them. Turning a corner, they saw the source. Two black eyes with slit pupils and rows of sharp bone-white teeth appeared in the darkness outside their light. The monster almost lazily came into view. It was about half the size of the tunnel. The body was reptilian, with gray scales that blended into the rock perfectly. Its thin tail waved slowly behind it as it leveled its gaze on the humans.

The drake opened its maw, and a white-hot stream of fire devoured the shadows hungrily, heading for Nyzir and Sinera. Moving quickly, Nyzir waved his halberd upward, and a wall of crystal shot up from the ground to the ceiling for a few seconds before the crystals shattered like glass. Sinera, remembering her water skin, summoned a jet of water that struck the fire stream. An explosion of steam flew everywhere. Grabbing his sister, Nyzir ran back to where they had come. The roar of the drake told them it was hot on their heels.

Looking around frantically, Nyzir saw what appeared to be a side passageway. It would be a tight squeeze, only allowing one person at a time. Sinera went first, with Nyzir not far behind. The drake snapped at them, but they were out of reach. It was about to breathe fire when, with a yelp of pain, the drake was yanked to the right. Nyzir and Sinera held their breath as the sound of crunching bone and torn scales was heard before it died down.   Nyzir slowly peered through the gap. There was the sound of scraping skin against rock as something large moved toward their hiding spot. Pulling out his crystal, Nyzir illuminated the scene. Something moved through the tunnel. First, he saw a mouth full of large sword-length teeth, with dark blood dribbling onto the stone. Then as it moved past, Nyzir saw pale flesh as the thing slithered away. Its bulk was as big as the tunnel itself. With dawning horror, Nyzir realized what must have created these tunnels. The drake, which was a cousin of the extinct dragon race, had been eaten by a wyrm. After a few seconds, the wyrm disappeared down the tunnel.

Glancing at his sister, Nyzir saw she was shaking. Tears were streaming down her face. Before Nyzir could speak, Sinera whispered, "What are we going to do? We can't even stop a drake, let alone that wyrm." After a pause, she continued, "I can't lose you, Nyzir. You're my only brother, and I feel like I'm not strong enough to protect—"

Sinera gasped as she was slapped across the face by her brother. She landed in a heap on the ground before Nyzir got on his knees, grabbed Sinera's face, and forced her to look at him. Nyzir had a fire in his eyes Sinera hadn't seen before, and he was trembling too.

"Don't you ever say that again. You hear me?" Nyzir took a breath before continuing. "Yes, we couldn't defeat that drake and certainly not the wyrm, but if we train harder and master our magic and fighting ability, we can defeat anything. Most importantly, like Sevastian said, we must be able to have each other's backs, meaning I'll always be there for you, and I know you'll be there for me when I need help. That's what siblings do, after all." Nyzir gripped Sinera and pulled her into a comforting hug. "Now are you with me and agree to support me even as I do you?" Nyzir said after breaking the embrace and stretched out his hand.

Sinera hesitated before a similar fire erupted in her eyes. She grasped his hand tightly and said, "I will always be there for you, whether to protect you from these beasts or even from yourself, if need be."

They grinned at each other before looking around the cavern. The only noteworthy thing was what appeared to be a stone sarcophagus in the middle of the cavern. The coffin itself was made of the same stone as the tunnels and was inlaid with various symbols. Nyzir and Sinera approached the coffin, and when they touched the stone, a shock of magic sent them both flying into the wall.

Grunting from the pain, Sinera walked back to the coffin, focused her magic into her hands, and touched the stone. When no shock came, she pushed the lid off. The stone lid fell to the ground with a resounding boom. Nyzir and Sinera's eyes widened.

Lying in the coffin was a man who looked like he had died yesterday. His skin was pale, a sharp contrast to his oak-brown hair and goatee. His thin frame was hidden under a black jerkin, and over his shoulders was a white bear fur cloak. His trousers and boots were dark gray. Clasped to his chest was a brown book, while to his side was a naked single-edged blade. His handsome face had a relaxed look as though he was merely sleeping.

Nyzir hesitantly touched the man's face. Instead of the cold of death, his skin felt slightly warm. Sinera reached over and carefully extracted the book from the man's hands. It looked unassuming—brown leather, not overly thick, and about the size of an adult hand. The cover only had three words: <u>Arinn the Hurricane</u>.

"Is that this guy's name?" Nyzir asked curiously.

Looking skeptical, Sinera attempted to open the book, but it wouldn't budge. Suddenly, little words appeared on the bottom of the cover. "Use the method with which you opened my tomb," it read. Eyes widening, Sinera funneled magic to her hands, and the book opened. Nyzir looked over her shoulder as she read.

First, I want to say to whomever is reading this, good job finding my resting place in these godforsaken tunnels. I suppose you've earned my respect and my legacy. My name is Arinn the Hurricane. I was one of the first ten to have magic. To not bore you, I'll explain simply.

I and my companions fought the only elder dragon that had taken this large blot of land as its own. My companions and I were beaten within an inch of our lives, and the elder dragon set us ablaze. However, when the flames disappeared, we only had light burns. We felt new energy coursing through us, and as the beast attacked, I swung my sword, and a dark gale blasted the dragon away. My friends also showed unusual abilities. They used heat, the earth, water from the lake, and others to drive back the dragon.

I called forth a massive gale that caused the dragon to fly out of control before using the wind to pierce its heart. As it died, we knew we could use this power over the elements to save our race. I took the title Arinn the Hurricane for my feat that day.

Over the decades, we built a city to hold us and to protect our loved ones. We named it Minraz. In that city, I had two sons and a daughter. All three had my magic, so I believed that our power could be passed down and our descendants could protect themselves from our enemies.

However, I still felt the malicious aura in the air that the elder dragon had radiated. Even as I lie here, dying of an illness, I feel its presence in the air. It hungers for revenge. I cannot stop it, and neither can my friends. We will entrust our legacy to you. Take my sword. It is woven with silver, so it is extra sharp against a monster's hide, and I found it channels winds even stronger than what I can summon.

— Arinn

CHAPTER 8

Closing the journal, they looked at the small book with the reverence of a holy relic.

"This is fantastic," Nyzir breathed. "Just think of what we can learn about our history and magic from this alone. It would be like he was teaching us himself."

Sinera had a similar look of awe before turning to Arinn's corpse. "What should we do with the blade?"

"I think I should use it, sis," Nyzir cut in. "After all, if it works like Arinn said, it should bolster my magic."

Reaching down, Nyzir carefully extracted the sword and sheath from Arinn's tomb. Looking closer, he saw in the light thick streaks of silver spider webbing through the dark metal. The sword itself was a bit long but workable. Strapping the scabbard to his hip, he sheathed the blade. Nyzir swiftly walked to the mouth of the entrance, pressed a hand to the tunnel, and closed his eyes. After a minute, Nyzir released a sigh of relief.

"At least it appears that wyrm has moved on. I don't fancy being lunch," he joked. "I suggest we move deeper into the tunnels, see what else we can find before finding our way back to the surface." He had that gleam in his citrine eyes that told Sinera his mischievous side would never die. "Come on, sis. Let's see what trouble we can find." Grabbing her arm, he led her back into the tunnel.

Sinera really wanted to say that any trouble they found might try to eat them but couldn't as she was led deeper into the tunnels. The walls and ground were slick with blood and slime from the wyrm, making navigating a chore. After many more twists and side passages, the siblings found something that stole their breath. An enormous cavern stood before them. It was even larger than the empress's throne room. Stalactites and stalagmites were aplenty here. On several occasions, they merged to create pillars to support the structure. This paled to what they saw at the far end of the cavern. A large waterfall was flowing into a lake that took up a third of the cavern.

As the siblings approached the waterfall, they found a cave in the wall next to it. The inside smelled of decaying animals, accompanied by the sound of snarling and teeth sinking into meat. Their glow crystals illuminated a large hairy form hunched in a corner, devouring something. After a second, the thing slowly turned around while snarling at the intrusion. It was a werewolf. It snarled, showing white teeth stained with red. Its fur and claws were also stained with blood. However, its eyes were what drew their attention. One eye was bright gold, while the other one was pink. Suddenly, he started convulsing and shied away from the siblings.

In a guttural voice, the werewolf spoke. "Whaattarreehumannss doinnggherree? Yoouuneedd too leavveebeforreeattacckk."

They tensed as the werewolf began convulsing before he stood to his full height. He towered over the siblings, forcing them to look up. Then he pounced, claws outstretched, teeth gnashing at the thought of blood. Nyzir and Sinera rolled out of the way of the werewolf as it skidded to a halt, head turning this way and that for its prey. Nyzir drew his sword without thinking, and the werewolf's eyes widened in shock.

"Silvveerrrr!" he growled.

He suddenly lunged at Nyzir with renewed vigor. Instinctively, Nyzir slashed with the blade, and a blast of wind threw the werewolf against the wall. Something nudged his mind and seemed to control his arm as he pointed the blade at the werewolf. Crystals rose from the earth and encased the werewolf.

Sinera approached the crystal statue warily as Nyzir joined her. "Do you think he's dead?" Sinera asked her brother.

Nyzir touched the crystal and focused on the werewolf. He felt blood pumping and a steady pulse. "He's alive, though I'm not sure what to do with him. He didn't seem to want to attack us. It was like he was taken over by his beast or something."

"I noticed he didn't like the silver in your sword," Sinera interjected. "Maybe the silver can repress his bloodlust."

Nyzir stared at the blade in thought before nodding. He placed the sword on the ground and put his finger two inches from the tip. Here, the problem rose. It was highly encouraged that you use a weapon to channel your magic as it made it easier in the heat of battle. However, Sevastian used his heat one-handed, so he might be able to as well.

He focused on making a blade of wind. When he used either the halberd or sword with wind, it felt like he was connected with the wind. Now it was like there was a brick wall between them. He closed his eyes and focused on destroying the wall. After a few seconds, cracks appeared in the wall. Nyzir concentrated harder, and more cracks were made. This time, Nyzir willed a large fist and smashed it against the wall in abandon.

After several strikes, the wall crumbled, and the wind soared, threw his body, and caressed him in its embrace. Nyzir's eyes opened, and he saw a wire-thin blade of wind an inch from his finger. With a grunt of triumph, Nyzir swiftly sliced two sections off the blade tip. With a smile, Nyzir opened his pack and pulled out a blanket. He sliced two strips off and took them to the statue. Nyzir pulled out the shorter sword and tapped it to the crystal that encased the werewolf's arms.

"I'm sorry," he whispered before strapping the silver-laced metal to the werewolf's arms.

The werewolf's eyes bulged as he tried to shake from the crystal. Nyzir put his hand on the arm and rubbed soothingly. A few minutes passed before the thrashing stopped. Nyzir warily shattered the crystals, and the werewolf dropped in a heap. After several gasping breaths, the werewolf looked at the humans. Its eyes were now both pink with slits in them.

"Whaatthappeneedd toomee?"

"I was able to apparently repress your bloodlust through the silver strapped on you," Nyzir said tiredly. The will that he had used for the magic had drained him.

"Yoouuhavveemyythankkss, humaann," the werewolf said.

"Can you help us find a way out of here?" Sinera asked.

"I caannhellppyoouufoorrwhaattyoouudiiddfoorrmee. Myynammeeiss Dyccee."

"Thank you, Dyce. You may lead us," Sinera said while grabbing Nyzir to help him.

Dyce led the siblings out of the cave, drank from the lake, and led them out of the cavern. The route was a long one as they had to sneak past a couple of monsters and even hide from another wyrm. After what felt like several hours, they escaped.

When they got out of the tunnel, they saw Sevastian flowing through a series of strikes. His movements looked honed from years of dedicated training as he flowed like water in a stream through offensive and defensive postures. Sevastian ducked an imaginary blade before impaling his sword where the body would have been. They watched as he hacked his way through the demons of imagination as he swung, sidestepped, and finally slew his enemies.

Suddenly, Sevastian stiffened. They heard him take several deep breaths. The only warning was the rising temperature before Sevastian waved his hand, and Nyzir and Sinera went flying to the right just as a ball of heat was thrown at Dyce. Dyce dived out of the way but received a powerful kick to the abdomen from Sevastian, which staggered him. Not wasting a second, Sevastian knocked Dyce to the ground and had his broadsword at Dyce's throat. However, before he could kill Dyce, his arms were strapped to his sides by ropes of water. Sinera was staggering to her feet, with her bow pointed at Sevastian.

"Don't kill him!" she shouted.

Sevastian looked at her with a mix of amusement and seriousness. Then suddenly, heat swept around his body in waves, and the water ropes evaporated into the air. Nyzir too looked ready to shout but stopped when he saw his master's expression.

"I will only ask once," Sevastian stated coldly. "Why is there a werewolf with you?"

"We found him in a cave," Nyzir said quickly. "But I was able to stop his bloodlust with the metal strapped to his arms. See?"

He pointed to Dyce's arms, and Sevastian noticed the silver-laced metal on his arms. An eyebrow rose before he sheathed his blade and stood back. Dyce gingerly got to his feet before moving toward the tunnel entrance.

"Wait, where are you going?" Nyzir looked at Dyce questioningly.

"Myyplacceeiss innthesseetunnellss. Iwiillalwayyss beegratefuullfoorr whaattyou'vveegiveennmee."

As he turned to return to his home, Sevastian spoke. "What is your name?"

"Dyccee," Dyce growled out.

"Dyce," Sevastian replied. "I'll be sure to remember that."

With that, Dyce dashed back into the tunnels.

Chapter 9

Looking at his students, Sevastian said sternly, "That was a risky gamble, you two!" Then his eyes softened. "Though I would have done the same. Remember, not all monsters are as they appear." With that, he gestured them to their mounts. As they got on and began trotting, Sevastian finally asked, "Nyzir, where did you get that sword?"

Before Nyzir could respond, his sister replied, "We found it in a tomb we discovered while hiding from a wyrm." She shuddered at the memory. "In the tomb was a man who had a journal with him, and it said he was Arinn the Hurricane, one of the first ten to have magic," she said quickly.

Sevastian raised an eyebrow before gesturing for the book. Fumbling in her pack, Sinera extracted the book and handed it to her master. Sevastian flipped through the pages quickly, eyes darting right and left so quickly that it made Nyzir nauseous. Finally, he closed the book and handed it back to Sinera.

In a revered voice, he said, "Don't let anyone take that book. I would study it as much as you can, especially you, Nyzir." He jerked a thumb at the journal. "That book can seriously help you with your wind training."

Sinera asked, "Master, where are we going now?"

"Right now, we're going to a mystic watchtower that we haven't heard from in a couple of weeks," Sevastian said shortly.

While they rode, the landscape and sky looked to be separated by a pane of glass. As the sun sent comforting warmth through Nyzir, Sinera reached in her pack and gave Nyzir a parcel.

"Here. You should eat this," she said with concern in her blue eyes.

Taking it, Nyzir found what looked like well-cooked steak. Taking a hesitant bite, he found the raw flavor of overcooked meat that was actually not bad. After gorging himself on half of it, he said, "This is pretty good, sis. What is It?"

Sinera gave a mischievous smile before saying slyly, "That, brother, is overcooked chimera that you and master prepared for us. While you were knocked out, Sevastian and I packaged what we could for the road. Enjoy!"

Nyzir gazed at the meat with piqued interest before inhaling the rest. They continued traveling north when an idea popped into Nyzir's mind. Looking at the blade at his hip, he thought about the ease with which he had summoned his wind, and with that thought came a name.

"I will name you Tempest. I think Arinn would approve of a storm to shield those who guard his legacy."

Sevastian quirked an eyebrow. "Interesting name but appropriate, I suppose."

After several hours of travel through grassy plains, they found a riverbank where they watered the unicorns. Squinting against the rising sun, Sevastian noticed something far along the bank that resembled a tower. Grinning, he gestured Nyzir and Sinera to come, and when they did, they too saw the tower.

Sevastian led his students to the tower. When they arrived, Nyzir gripped Tempest's hilt tightly and swore quietly. The front of the tower was black from char. A man with no legs and a hole in his forehead lay sprawled on the grass. Two more bodies had been roasted alive, leaving nothing recognizable. The final two were severed from the torso.

Sevastian looked at the scene with hard eyes before he strode to the man with the hole in his forehead. Bending down, Sevastian closed the man's eyes before inspecting the remaining four. When he returned, Sevastian's eyes were harder than steel.

"I'm going to enter the tower. You two try and move the bodies by the lake."

Without waiting for a reply, he spun around and entered the watchtower. The inside was as bad as he had feared. Most of the room was black from burned-out flames. However, there was a less-charred spot near the bunks.

He paused and glanced at his students. They were heaving the corpses together with some difficulty. The way Nyzir and Sinera worked together, both in combat and out of combat, brought envy to his heart. It reminded him of days that felt like an eternity ago when he had had—

No! Sevastian clenched his fist tightly as the unwanted memories assaulted him. *Maybe that's why I was assigned to them.* The thought ran through his mind. Taking a deep breath, Sevastian forced his body to relax. He swiftly searched the beds and found nothing.

Growling, Sevastian then went up the stairs to find one last body. Though he had been burned to death, Sevastian saw that he was young, seventeen at most. The terror in his eyes was burned into Sevastian's mind. Taking a breath, he carefully closed his eyes and lifted the man in his arms. He took him out of the tower to see Nyzir and Sinera moving the last body. With a sigh, Sevastian strode toward them and carefully placed the teen's body with those of his companions.

The three of them stood, heads bowed in respect, before a shadow encased them. Before they could move, they were knocked off their feet and pinned down by something large and scaly. Stars blazed across Nyzir's vision before he finally saw a giant monster holding him down. His eyes widened in shock as he saw the beast that he had only heard about in his mother's nighttime stories. It was a dragon.

The dragon itself was beautiful in a deadly way. Blood-red scales gave way to ivory-white talons and teeth pressed in a snarl as it swung its huge head back and forth among the three it had pinned. The dragon's yellow eyes locked with Nyzir's.

Humans, know that for now, I will not rip you apart. I only wish to speak. The dragon's voice, high but clear, sliced through Nyzir's mind with the keenness of Tempest's edge. Sevastian and Sinera looked shocked by the speech before the dragon turned its head to Sevastian.

I bear a warning for you and your hatchlings. I have been tasked by my sire to attack your settlement. But I tire of being his pawn for his revival. So will you help me retain my free will, or should I slaughter you and search for another? Sevastian looked shocked. He tried to look away, but the dragon caught his eye every time. Seeing no other option under the circumstances, he snarled, "Say we listen to you. What do you want of us?"

Good. Listening is a valuable instinct human. I have thought long about my plan, but I need your word of agreement before I explain. If you agree, we can stop my sire before he regains his old strength. All I'll need from you is some of your magic.

"Say we agree to your plan," Sevastian replied with narrowed eyes. "How long would we have to prepare before your attack?"

The dragon paused for a moment as if considering if Sevastian's question was worth answering. *The attack will be in two moons' time. There will be an assortment of beasts that will attack as well. I need to make it look convincing to not arouse suspicion. So I ask again—will you agree?* The dragon then lifted its forelegs into the air, and Sevastian, Nyzir, and Sinera scrambled to their feet before facing the dragon.

Sevastian was still hesitant. "Why should we trust an overgrown lizard? For all we know, you could be lying through your teeth."

Take my warning or leave it, human, the dragon snarled. *Do you wish to survive and prosper or be used for petty amusement by my sire and eventually removed from this world?*

Sevastian looked at Nyzir and Sinera before he gave a slight nod, which seemed to satisfy the dragon.

The dragon growled, *I will collect some of your magic after the battle to revive my sire. The revival will take time and preparation. During that time, he is at his weakest. Your power will be all I need to end him."* With that, the dragon launched itself skyward before flying off.

Nyzir stared with awe and fear in his eyes. "If he's that powerful," Nyzir whispered, "how can we expect to stop his father if he is revived?"

"Master, I think we should assume what that dragon said to be true. We need to alert Empress Sylia!" Sinera exclaimed.

Sevastian closed his eyes, breathed deeply, and, upon opening his eyes, looked upon the corpses of the mystics stationed at the watchtower. His fist clenched and unclenched before speaking. "I too believe his story. This means I need to get us up north as fast as the wind may carry us."

Chapter 10

Icy gusts tore at Nyzir's coat with abandon as he, along with Sinera and Sevastian, trudged through the thigh-deep snow of a mountain pass. They had been forced to leave the unicorns at a small town before trekking through the northern mountains. While Nyzir managed to use his wind magic to somewhat stifle the worst of the wind, it did nothing for the cold that was determined to seep into his bones. Sevastian, however, was encased in a faint red outline as he battled the wind. Nyzir noted his master's face was trying to remain impassive. However, the strain of using his magic to maintain warmth was causing creases in his forehead.

Despite the icy wind, Nyzir noted that the mountains held a certain beauty. The sun illuminated the snow, forcing Nyzir to avert his gaze. Something black flashed by, and he saw it was his sister's hair snapping in the gale. Nyzir's eyes followed his sister's hair. He gave himself a mental shake. She was his sister, for Arinn's sake. As he thought back to what Sevastian had said about mystic relationships, it didn't sound so crazy.

I'll worry about this later, Nyzir thought as they left the pass behind, only to stumble in a cave to escape the biting wind.

Once inside, Sevastian started a small fire, while Nyzir and Sinera unloaded a few snow rabbits they had hunted. After eating, Sevastian extracted his bedroll from his pack.

"We'll leave when the wind dies down a bit," Sevastian mumbled tiredly. "For now, I advise you two get some rest." With that, he drifted off.

Sinera quickly joined her master, leaving Nyzir the role of sentry, which he didn't mind. He leaned back against the wall of the cave and looked at Sinera. She had a small smile on her face, which brought one to Nyzir's own. Sevastian, however, was frowning, with his brows crinkling.

As Sevastian turned over, he muttered, "Why'd you do it? You had no reason to," before showing Nyzir his back and falling deeper into sleep.

Nyzir raised an eyebrow at his master's words before deciding to ask him later. Out of boredom, he drew Tempest and examined it for damage, but there was none. The blade was as sharp and beautiful as it must have been when freshly forged. Nyzir could feel the wind magic pulsing faintly through the blade, a constant reminder that it wouldn't fail him. While not an expert on weapon forging, Nyzir at least knew that for Tempest to have the wind magic it had, it required the forger to infuse said magic into the metal during the forging. Weapons of this sort were rare as the way to make a magically enhanced weapon was a secretive art. As such, Nyzir would never relinquish Tempest. He would become as skilled with the sword as with his halberd. As darkness crept through the cave, Nyzir decided a nap wouldn't hurt since the wind was as strong as ever. Closing his eyes, he slept soundly.

The thing that had awoken Nyzir was unexpected to him. A faint voice, carried by the wind, whistled into Nyzir's ear. He slowly stood, grabbing Tempest, and hid next to the cave entrance. He strained his ear and caught the voice again. It was feminine, probably a little older than he was.

"Stupid twins messing up the floor again. I don't see why we have to watch them while their father's hunting." A sigh was faintly heard. "Well, at least I have my cave, where I can be by myself for a bit."

Nyzir thought he heard a smile in her voice as he heard what must have been her crunching through the snow. Nyzir glanced at his sister and mentor before taking a breath and stepped out of the cave. Maybe this woman could help them find the ice tribes, which was Nyzir's mental reasoning for going to meet the woman.

The wind, while not as bad as earlier, still forced Nyzir to squint slightly at the approaching figure. She appeared slightly taller than him, though that may have been her clothing. From what Nyzir could tell, the woman's garments looked to be composed of different animal skins and furs. He could make out rabbit, fox, and even wolf fur.

The woman stiffened and then, with speed that shouldn't be possible in this snow, was in Nyzir's face in a few sharp bounds. As Nyzir raised his arms in some form of peace, the woman ducked, grabbed his ankle, and forced him into the snow face-first. She flipped him over and had a single-edged dagger at his throat before Nyzir could blink. As they stared at each other, Nyzir became lost in the woman's eyes. They were an icy blue that held an equal amount of mischief and determination as they drilled into Nyzir's own. Her mouth pulled back in a snarl, giving Nyzir a view of teeth filed to slight points. Despite the predicament he was in, Nyzir couldn't stop thinking about how exotic they looked.

"What are you doin' in my cave?" the woman breathed. She spoke with a slight accent, though Nyzir couldn't place it.

Trying to appear nonchalant despite his pounding heart, Nyzir replied, "You see, I, my sister, and my mentor were staying till the wind died down enough for us to continue. We're searching for the ice tribes. Could you maybe point us in the right direction? Then we'll leave, and we won't have to see each other again."

The woman's eyes widened as she felt something poking her rib. Glancing down, she saw a dagger pointed at her kidney. Nyzir's eyes adopted a mischievous quality.

"Besides," Nyzir drawled as smoothly as he could, "it would be a waste to hurt such a pretty woman as you, no?"

The woman smirked, leaned forward, and whispered in Nyzir's ear. "I'll admit you're not bad looking, but does that really get you any, where you come from?"

"Well, now that you mention it," Nyzir said calmly. He hoped Sinera or Sevastian noticed his absence, but so far, it appeared not. Nyzir would have to use what charm he had to escape. "You never did answer my question, and I think your name might be nice as well. Seeing as we're having such a lovely chat," Nyzir said in what he thought was a charming voice.

Smiling, the woman again leaned into Nyzir's ear and whispered, "Kat is my name. As for if I know the ice tribes, I might know a few members you could meet. What are you offering in exchange?" Kat leaned back and gave Nyzir a sultry look.

Before Nyzir could respond, Sinera's voice sliced through the air. "Your life—unless you'd rather get off my brother and help us."

Kat and Nyzir looked to see Sinera standing, with her bow drawn and an arrow pointing at Kat. Shrugging, Kat got off Nyzir and offered him a hand. Hesitantly, Nyzir grasped it, and she pulled him upright.

As he stood, he pulled Kat close and whispered, "Name's Nyzir. So you know, that's my sister, Sinera." With that, he grabbed Kat's arm not too gently and led her back into the cave.

When the trio entered, they saw Sevastian standing with his arms folded and staring intently at them.

Nyzir flinched slightly under his teacher's gaze before gesturing at Kat. "This is Kat. She says she can get us to the ice tribes."

Sevastian inclined his head slightly before turning his gaze to Kat. Nyzir was impressed, albeit grudgingly, that Kat could keep Sevastian's stare with one of her own.

They stared at each other for several seconds before she blurted out, "I can take you three to the tribes. I swear. Just don't kill me."

Sevastian studied her as a miner would study jewels before his gaze softened slightly. He put a hand on Kat's shoulder and said, "That's all I ask of you, Kat. Who knows? Maybe you could be a good influence on my students. You know, let them see what life is like outside of Minraz."

Kat looked confused before shrugging. These three weren't going to kill her, so she might as well cooperate. "Yeah, that's fine and all," Kat replied finally. "But we won't be able t'leave for awhile. The wind's still mad as a baby-laden woman out there."

However, to the shock of everyone present, the wind died down significantly as the words left Kat's mouth. Kat's eyes widened and then narrowed slightly as she thought she knew what had happened. The ice tribes did have a deity. It was said that their goddess watched over their frozen home with the tenacity of a mother watching her child. Though Kat had not even seen the goddess, she had been instructed to recognize her signs of intervention in the world, and this assuredly was one of them.

Turning back to the other occupants of the cave, she gestured outside impatiently. "What are you three standing there gawking for? Let's get going before the blasted wind comes back." With that said, she nudged Nyzir sharply, and he, Sinera, and Sevastian quickly packed up their belongings, and they sprinted out of the cave.

As the snow seemed undecided as to whether to be firm or soft, Nyzir had to carefully adjust his weight from foot to foot as he moved along the path. Glancing up, he saw Kat moving with a practiced grace that seemed natural. Sevastian was moving carefully as well but with more confidence than Nyzir as he moved to catch up. Sinera, though slightly uneasy at first, was soon matching her brother in keeping up with Kat.

Kat glanced toward Sevastian before addressing him. "So why do you three want t' get to the tribes? Can't imagine it's for the scenery. I also need to know what you're called."

Sevastian thought about if he should tell this, for all intents and purposes, stranger about their plan. He shook his head slightly. He was going to have to tell people anyway, so what the hell? "Sinera needs training in ice magic, so that's why we're here, and my name is Sevastian." He waited for her to respond.

Kat looked intrigued. "So she"—Kat pointed at Sinera—"can manipulate ice like we can? Then does that mean all of you can manipulate elements? I've heard rumors, of course, but never seen someone use elements other than our ice." All this came out of Kat in a rush, her eyes gleaming in excitement as she glanced from the three of them to back to the path.

Nyzir, seeing an opportunity to see ice magic in action, stepped up and said, "How 'bout this, Kat? You show us your magic, and I'll show you mine."

Kat looked at him with amusement before she reached down to the snow. When her hand was a foot from the ground, the snow started to shift and move as though something was pushing through it until, incredibly, a rose made of ice pushed its way out of the snow to stand tall four inches above the snow. With a grin on her face, Kat gently plucked the ice flower from the ground. It even had miniature thorns on the stem. She gave it to Nyzir carefully.

Nyzir felt slight goosebumps as their hands touched before he inspected the rose. Its shape and structure were perfect. The petals looked identical to those of roses Nyzir had seen in gardens in Minraz. With a smile, Nyzir attempted to hand Kat the rose, but she stopped him with a raised hand.

"It's yours now," Kat said simply. "Don't worry 'bout it melting. Our ice never melts unless we will it. Now it's your turn," she finished with expectance written on her face.

Seeing the opportunity to mess with their guide/friend, Nyzir drew Tempest, the setting sun nearly blinding him by reflecting off the blade. Nyzir pointed Tempest's tip at the ground and focused. After a few seconds, a daisy made of multicolored crystal rose from the snow. The center was the same blue as Kat's eyes, while the petals were a variety of red, green, and even pink. With a smile, Nyzir picked up the flower and presented it to Kat.

Her eyes were wide and her mouth slightly ajar as she tentatively took the daisy. Holding it as if it would break any moment, she inspected the flower. She had only seen this flower once when she was exploring a cave that had a water spring when she was young. The flower Nyzir had given her matched the daisy she'd seen perfectly.

A way to thank Nyzir sprang up in her mind, and a coy smile graced her lips. Carefully putting the daisy in a pouch, she walked up to Nyzir and, with a slight tinge of pink on her face, pecked Nyzir on the cheek before stepping back. Nyzir's eyes widened as heat swept threw him. Sinera's eyes, however, narrowed dangerously. She didn't know what this woman saw in her brother, but if she thought she could lead him along, Kat would find an arrow between her eyes.

Sevastian looked nonplused by the display until he saw Sinera's reaction. *Well, this could be interesting* was the thought that ran through Sevastian's head.

Kat spoke up then, her voice slightly hushed. "Thank you, Nyzir. This means a lot to me."

With that, they continued their movement through the snow. They traveled fairly quickly, saving their breath for speed, but Nyzir still looked about the scenery with interest. Several times, they passed trees stripped of their leaves. He saw white foxes hunting smaller game, only to flee at their approach. With the blanket of white over everything and the crispness of the air, Nyzir felt contentment settle into his gut. The peace the northern mountains represented was a nice contrast to the everyday hubbub of Minraz. Nyzir hoped everyone back home was preparing. Sevastian had sent a messenger bird to Minraz warning them to evacuate the civilians and prepare for the battle in two moons.

After about an hour of moving, Nyzir noted something about Kat. With each step as they caressed a large hill, Kat would get tenser with each couple of steps. Nyzir opened his mouth to speak, but Kat raised a hand to silence him. Looking at Kat, Nyzir saw nervousness eating at her eyes but also a warning to not probe her.

When the group reached the top of the hill, Nyzir was left spellbound by what was below. In the shadow of a mountain lay a village the likes of which Nyzir had never seen. From the vantage point, he could see that every slightly shabby-looking house was made of ice. The houses themselves were small, only one story, but with apparently enough room for the occupants. They were, however, placed with no real order in mind as Nyzir saw people swerving in between the houses to wherever they went. A chuckle sounded from his right, and Nyzir saw Kat grinning at him.

"Might not be too pretty," Kat drawled out, "but it's home. Come on." With that, she carefully slid down the hill, looked back, and gestured them down.

Nyzir glanced at Sinera and Sevastian. They looked at him as if to say, "Well, go on." Shrugging, Nyzir slid down the hill none too gracefully, with his sister and mentor hot on his heels.

As they approached the village, a group of ten rushed to meet them. They were garbed similarly to Kat, with a variety of weapons drawn, from daggers to short swords, and someone had what looked like a mace. After surrounding their quarry, one of the men approached. He was slightly taller than Sevastian, a sword gripped in his fist, but his clothing masked his features from Nyzir's view. As the man approached, he glowered at Kat. Kat, to Nyzir's shock, looked down at her feet before looking the man in the eye.

"Kat." The man's voice told Nyzir this man was in his fourth or fifth decade. "So you came back from your alone time, and you brought *friends*, did you?"

Kat looked uncomfortable but stayed her ground. "Father," Kat spoke softly, "these three wanted to meet with you about helping Sinera with ice manipulation." Kat gestured to Sinera as she spoke.

Kat's father looked at Sinera critically. Sinera looked back. Finally, Kat's father sighed and lowered his sword. "You four will have to be taken to the ice sages. They will decide your fate."

The men then led them through the village. Nyzir noted the populace giving them glances of both curiosity and hostility, though no one said anything. As Nyzir passed some houses, he noticed lots of intricate designs in the ice, from snowflakes to pictures of the various animals to be found here. As they weaved past houses, Kat finally lowered her hood. Her hair, which, Nyzir guessed, reached her back, was the same color as her eyes.

Kat caught Nyzir staring and smiled at him. "Don't worry, Nyzir. I'm used to it." Kat spoke calmly as they walked.

"So you know, your hair is quite . . . exotic. I like it."

She flashed Nyzir a smile.

Kat's father decided to speak then. "Daughter, taking a liking to this boy, are ya?" There was a slight edge in his voice as he spoke.

"Come now, Yorou. She's old enough to decide what she wants," spoke the man next to him.

Yorou grunted but kept his peace before they reached the base of the mountain. Nyzir saw a worn path leading up the mountain. They could only walk in groups of four as they walked the path. After several minutes, they arrived at a cave entrance. There was a bell outside embedded in the mountainside. Yorou rang the bell three times and waited.

Before long, a man's voice said, "Only your daughter and the guests may enter."

Without a word, Yorou ushered Kat, Nyzir, Sinera, and Sevastian inside. After they entered, a sheet of ice flowed across the cave mouth, blocking the wind and any escape they might try. They moved deeper into the cave. Several fires erupted from hidden pots around them. But these fires were bluish white rather than orange. They gave the cave an ethereal glow as they illuminated five figures seated in intricate chairs made of ice. They were all garbed in white robes with blue filigree. Their heads were bare, showing the five to be from their mid-thirties to early fifties.

The man in the center, who looked to be in his fourth decade, if the shallow lines in his face proved anything, said in a voice that held Nyzir's attention, "Please sit, guests. You must have traveled a long way to stand before us." He waved what looked like a staff made of white wood, and four plain ice chairs grew from ground.

After they were seated, the man gestured to himself. "We are the ice sages. My name is Prak, and I wish to hear your reasons for coming here."

Sevastian opened his mouth and told Prak a shorter version of their tale, highlighting the threat they had come across and Sinera's need for instruction. After the tale, Prak looked thoughtful before turning his black eyes to Kat.

"You did well, child, to bring these three to us. However, while I detect no ill intent from them, we cannot train an outsider without—" He froze as the bell outside rang quickly. Looking annoyed at the interruption, Prak waved his staff, and the ice melted away. A youth, possibly a little older than Nyzir and similarly garbed as the ice sages, dashed inside.

"Honorable sages," the youth panted out, "*she* wants to meet with that girl." He gestured to Sinera.

Prak, looking between thoughtful and concerned, said gravely, "Very well. Take her to where she must go."

Nodding, the youth turned to Sinera. "Quickly, miss. Mustn't keep her waiting."

Nyzir was about to speak, but Kat whispered. "She'll be fine. Let her go."

Nyzir looked conflicted but kept his mouth shut. Sinera rose and, after an encouraging nod from Kat, followed the youth outside. They passed Yorou without comment and ascended the mountain path.

After a few minutes, the youth, seeming to think Sinera was nervous, said, "Don't fret, miss. You have been chosen for a great honor."

Sinera replied dryly, "And what honor would that be?"

"You'll see," the youth said cryptically.

They continued for several minutes before reaching the entrance to a tunnel. Sinera looked at the tunnel and then at the young man.

He looked back evenly through pale brown eyes before he said seriously, "Remember, treat her with respect."

Before Sinera could ask why, the youth walked away without looking back. Fighting back a scowl, Sinera walked into the tunnel. The darkness seemed to swallow her whole. She blindly fumbled to the side of the tunnel to guide her. As she moved deeper into the tunnel, she saw something approach. An orb of white light, perhaps the size of an apple, gently floated toward Sinera. As it floated, the orb got slightly brighter before floating a foot from Sinera.

As she peered at the orb, a voice, feminine but brimming with confidence, said, "Come," and the orb floated down the tunnel.

Scrambling to keep up, Sinera followed the orb a bit before they arrived in a large cavern. The orb flew up to the ceiling and then brightened considerably, giving Sinera a clear view of everything around her. On every available wall surface were drawings, too many to count, everything from animals to epic battles, to ordinary things such as clouds and food.

At the far end of the cavern, a woman was humming a tune as she drew. Her long scarlet hair gleamed from the orb of light. She wore a white dress with cerulean and gold interwoven in patterns. The dress reached to her knees, showing Sinera bare feet.

Sinera, deciding to break the silence, said, "What are you doing?"

The woman, not stopping, replied jovially, "What does it look like, silly? I'm making a masterpiece. Come and give me your opinion."

The woman waved Sinera over. Hesitantly, she approached the strange woman. When Sinera was next to her, the woman turned her face to look

Sinera in the eye. She had a heart-shaped face. Her amethyst eyes glowed with eagerness at what Sinera thought. The woman looked to be in her early thirties, but it was hard to tell.

Looking at the drawing, Sinera saw it was an incredibly detailed dragon. While she had seen rough images in storybooks, the dragon on the wall outdid them in leaps and bounds. Sinera could see every scale on its hide. The great wings, spread out in flight, looked to eclipse the sun. The maw was letting loose a condensed stream of fire toward the sky as if to proclaim its majesty to the heavens.

"It's beautiful," Sinera whispered.

"You're too kind, young Sinera," the woman replied, smiling. "Drawing is such a lovely pastime when one is bored, isn't it?"

Sinera, not knowing how to respond, merely nodded.

"Excellent!" the woman exclaimed. "Now sit down with me, Sinera. We have much to discuss." She promptly sat down in a meditative position with her arms in her lap.

Sinera, with a look of confusion on her face, joined the woman. Sinera voiced something that had been eating her since she first met this woman. "What is your name? Why am I here talking to you?"

The woman merely looked at Sinera critically before replying. "Names are powerful things, young one. I will tell you mine if you've earned my trust. As for why you are here, could it be that an old woman just wants some company?" She chuckled at her own jest before looking back at Sinera.

"You don't look so old to me," Sinera answered back, "and that wasn't an answer to my question."

The woman blinked before an amused twinkle appeared in her eye. "Do not judge by appearance, for in truth, I guess you could consider me ageless. As for the answer, that depends on if you can be honest."

"Honest about what?" Sinera gnashed out at the woman's dodging of her questions.

"What is going on between you and that cute brother of yours?" the woman asked simply.

Sinera's eyes widened, and she sputtered out, "W-what are you talking about? There's nothing between us but blood."

"So you say," drawled out the woman. "Yet I feel your blood boil when the girl who found you talks to your brother. Hmmm."

Sinera looked shocked, opened her mouth, closed it again, and sagged in defeat. "You're right," Sinera whispered, "but I don't know what it means."

The woman looked sympathetic as she put a hand on Sinera's shoulder. "It's nothing to be ashamed of, dear. You two simply share a deeper bond than most. I am not offended, and neither should you be."

Sinera felt as if a great weight had been lifted.

"The reason I summoned you was also to meet you in person. You are the only magically gifted outside of these frozen plains to have ice in your veins. The reason for that is me." The woman pointed to herself for emphasis.

Sinera's eyes widened. "How are you the cause of my magic? It's unheard of for someone to be *given* magic by someone else."

The woman sighed and looked at Sinera with sad eyes. "I have been waiting for you since you were born, Sinera. You have your magic because I imparted to you the energy for the magic to take form when you were in your mother's womb. My influence beyond the frozen north is extremely limited. However, I hoped you would not be discouraged by your strange power, and you weren't, just like I hoped."

"Influence," Sinera said, disbelieving. "What are you, lost in the head, or are you some sort of creature with ice powers?"

"In a way," the woman replied. "Believe me or not, I am the winter goddess. I allowed you, your brother, and your mentor into my domain, a feat in and of itself, you know."

Sinera, looking skeptical, decided to see how this played out. "A goddess, huh? Well, nice to meet you," she finished, sticking out her hand in greeting.

The goddess burst out laughing at that. She laughed so hard, she had to brace herself on one arm. After she calmed down, the goddess grinned at Sinera. "What a breath of fresh air you are. Most just bow down, begging forgiveness or whatnot, and that gets so boring after a while."

"I can certainly understand." Sinera giggled, surprising herself at her joy.

The goddess lost her mirth as she locked eyes with Sinera. "I have something for you."

She reached into her dress and pulled out a necklace. It was a single miniature sword. Hanging next to it was a large snowflake. The goddess handed the necklace to Sinera, who tentatively put it on. When it touched her skin, Sinera felt cold fire running through her veins. The ice magic in her blood pulsed, and she felt it more acutely than ever. The welcome chill in her body was far from unpleasant.

The goddess smiled and, leaning forward, whispered in Sinera's ear, "Know that you carry my blessing, Sinera, and know that I am watching over you. Now I do believe you have earned my name. However, share it only with those you trust most, understand?"

Sinera nodded, overwhelmed by the trust this goddess had in her.

The goddess leaned into Sinera's ear and whispered so softly that Sinera almost missed it, "Micenta is my name. Now go and show the world the power of my ice."

With a smile, Micenta gently pulled Sinera into a hug. After a few seconds, they parted, with Sinera having a smile on her face before being led out by the orb of light. Sinera looked back to see Micenta back to drawing while humming that tune that only she knew. With newfound confidence, Sinera strode out of the cavern, ready to show the ice tribes what she could do.

CHAPTER 11

Nyzir shifted awkwardly in his chair as he waited for his sister. She had left several minutes ago, and it was getting awkward just sitting and waiting. Out of boredom, Nyzir, deciding to experiment on his magic, brought out a crystal the size of his hand. Furrowing his brows in concentration, Nyzir set about trying to shape the crystal. It was harder than he thought it would be. The crystal required more magic and mental focus to shape into something different. He slowly changed the crystal in his hand into a perfect sphere, and after some strain, he made it into a cube. It might have been easier to use more crystal, but Nyzir wanted to test his control.

While he shaped the crystal, the other occupants watched him with varying expressions. Sevastian was watching his student with a mix of amusement and pride. Kat was watching Nyzir with rapt fascination, eyeing the ever-changing crystal. The ice sages looked impressed by Nyzir's focus and even started whispering to one another in soft rapid tones. Nyzir felt eyes on himself, so he looked up at everyone watching him. Heat rose in his cheeks before he hesitantly put the crystal in his lap.

"This young man seems skilled to be able to shape crystal," spoke Prak with interest in his eyes.

Nyzir looked Prak in the eye before replying, "I don't think I'm that skilled. I'm still learning my elements, Sage Prak."

Prak replied respectively, "Nonsense, my boy. Do not sell yourself short. But what is this about 'elements'? Do you have more than one?"

Nyzir looked sheepish before he raised his other hand. After a moment, a mini cyclone rose from his hand, spinning as rapidly as a top. After a second, the cyclone dissipated into the air. Prak looked dumbstruck by the demonstration. His mouth moved as if he was talking to himself. Prak opened his mouth when the bell outside chimed. Prak's face changed to neutral so fast, Nyzir had to keep himself from laughing. After a wave of Prak's staff, Sinera entered, with the youth bowing before scurrying out of the cave.

Nyzir studied his sister. Her face showed happiness and determination as she approached Prak. When she walked past, Nyzir noticed a necklace he had never seen. It was a sword with a snowflake hanging next to it. Sinera flashed her brother a small smile before standing before the ice sages. She took off the necklace and handed it to Prak. As if he were holding a holy relic, Prak appraised the necklace, admiring it from every angle with a reverence that puzzled Nyzir. What could be so important about a necklace?

Prak returned it to Sinera and ushered her to seat. Nyzir now saw a look of wonder in Prak's eyes as he looked at them.

"Sinera, was it?" Prak addressed her.

Sinera nodded.

"Given that you possess that necklace, it is obvious you carry our goddess's favor."

Kat's eyes widened in shock, but she kept her silence.

Prak continued, "As such, we will train you in our ways. But be warned—the ice is as sharp as it is beautiful." Prak paused and then addressed Kat. "Kat, as you were the person who brought these three, they will stay with you." A twinkle of mirth appeared in his eye.

Kat opened her mouth to retort but, upon seeing Prak's gaze, closed it and stood stiffly. Nyzir, guessing this meant they were dismissed, stood, with Sinera and Sevastian following suit.

As they moved to the entrance, Prak spoke. "Know that I will be paying attention to you three. Do try not to disappoint me."

Nyzir and Sinera both turned to look Prak in the eye.

"Don't worry," Nyzir replied.

"We won't," Sinera finished.

Appearing satisfied, Prak gestured them out.

Upon reaching the base of the mountain, Kat and Yorou led their newly appointed guests through the village. People gave them suspicious glances but didn't seem bothered to speak up. After all, what could three people do against a whole village? While they navigated, Nyzir wondered if this place had a name.

When he voiced this, Kat chuckled and said, "While we never named our home, some people wanted it named after Iketh, one of the first to find this place and make it our home."

Nyzir grinned as they made their way to a house on the far side of Iketh. While it didn't look especially noteworthy, Nyzir noted a measure of comfort in the design. The house was a single story, big enough for a small family. When Yorou opened the door, Nyzir saw no discomfort as he gripped the ice knob. Curious, Nyzir reached out and touched it. To his shock, the ice wasn't cold, merely pleasantly cool.

Before he opened his mouth, Yorou spoke up. "As you know, our ice doesn't melt unless we will it. Now you also know that we can control the temperature of our ice." He walked on without looking back.

Nyzir, Sinera, and Sevastian entered the house and were surprised to find a large amount of furs covering the floors. Nyzir saw Yorou and Kat rummaging around in what appeared to be a kitchen, pulling out meat and bowls made of oak. While Yorou filled the bowls with snow water, Kat set about setting up seating areas. Her face was a mask of concentration as she worked to make a chair out of ice. Sinera approached Kat and whispered into her ear. Nyzir caught the words *help* and *ice*. Kat looked momentarily shocked before inclining her head and whispering back quickly. Nodding, Sinera pulled out her bow and began helping Kat.

After several minutes, five chairs were assembled around a small round table. Kat looked grateful, while Sinera had a calculating look before she shook her head fiercely and then sat down slowly. Yorou came in with five bowls of steaming soup. The smell made Nyzir's mouth water. The soup itself tasted delicious, with herbs Nyzir couldn't identify. Sinera and Sevastian had similar looks as they downed the food. When they finished, Yorou addressed them.

"Tomorrow morning you two"—he gestured at Nyzir and Sinera—"will spar against m'daughter here. Let me get an eye of your skill with those weapons. Also, as you are my guests, you three will help us with hunting. We're running low on food. Finally, I'll be teaching you, Sinera, to use ice. These chairs are a fine start, but you and my daughter both need serious instruction. Now off to bed with ya. There's a spare room on the right."

Nyzir lay on the surprisingly soft furs, trying to coax his body to sleep. His sister and mentor slept on. His last thought was that this trip was definitely going to be interesting.

CHAPTER 12

The chilly wind served as an effective way to properly wake up, Nyzir discovered, waiting with Sinera at their new training area, a fairly flat expanse of snowed-over land not far from Iketh. They had to wait a good five minutes before Sevastian, Yorou, and Kat approached. Of the three, Kat looked the most at ease, moving to stand beside Nyzir and Sinera, and waited for her father to speak. Yorou and Sevastian grinned at each other.

Yorou explained the instructions. "You three will engage in a weapons-only spar, meanin' no magic. However, you may still use any other tactic if you want." He winked at Kat, who groaned slightly, before he continued. "Nyzir, you will go first. Then Sinera. The spar ends when I say so. Also, wounds will teach you—but not if you can never recover. You will begin when I say."

He stepped back, while Sevastian gestured Sinera over by his side. Nyzir and Kat then faced each other. Kat had a confident smile while twirling her daggers. Nyzir simply drew Tempest and adopted a ready stance. Simultaneously, the two lunged forward. Kat began with a rapid series of jabs and swift slashes, while Nyzir parried and desperately shifted his body to evade.

The clang of metal on metal was music to Nyzir's ears as he maneuvered Tempest in a defensive pattern to block or redirect Kat's daggers. Already, he could tell he was at a disadvantage. Kat was quicker, and her daggers made it harder to defend. She apparently noticed too. With a wicked grin, she pressed her advantage. Nyzir blocked a strike, only to narrowly duck a fist to his face. Acting on instinct, he rammed his shoulder into Kat's midsection. Kat, however, rolled with the blow, only to be right back up.

She had a fire in her eyes as she stared at Nyzir. Suddenly, laughter erupted from Kat, a joyous melody that made Nyzir's heart skip a beat.

After a second, she calmed down enough to say, "You're not bad, Nyzir," before reengaging him. As their blades danced, she spoke up again, only loud enough for Nyzir to hear. "You know, Nyzir, my blades are thirsty for your blood." As she said those last words, she did indeed draw blood, a slash on Nyzir's right arm, a cut on the opposite cheek, and a shallow stab at his chest.

Nyzir grunted in pain as he backed off to breathe for a second. The stab wound hurt the most but not unbearably so. Kat smiled before she went stalking to Nyzir like a predator after its prey, only this prey could fight back. As she dashed to Nyzir, Kat saw him reach down for the snow on the ground. She quickly grabbed some herself before they hurled it in each other's faces.

Nyzir staggered back, desperately wiping snow from his eyes before he was tackled to the ground. Tempest flew from his hand while he and Kat rolled, desperately fighting for control. Nyzir seized one of Kat's daggers as he pinned her beneath him. He pressed the flat of the blade against her throat, but Kat wasn't done. She drew up a knee in an attempt to hit Nyzir's crotch, which only partially connected because of Nyzir's pinning her legs with his own. It still hurt though. Involuntary tears sprang from Nyzir's eyes as he pressed the dagger harder into Kat's neck. Kat, managing to twist her arm enough, pressed her other dagger to Nyzir's throat. His eyes widened before they locked onto Kat's. They glared before hearing Yorou's voice.

"All right, you two, I say it's a draw. Now up ya get, and get over here."

Nyzir and Kat stood up together, each eyeing the other warily. The thrill of battle had left them, leaving them tired but exhilarated. Nyzir walked passed Yorou to stand by Sevastian—but not before receiving a nod of respect from the man. Sevastian gave Nyzir an encouraging smile before doing the same for Sinera.

Adopting a blank look, Sinera approached Kat. A silent challenge was raised between the two as they readied themselves. Sinera quickly drew an arrow and let it fly at Kat, but Kat dodged effortlessly before dashing to her new opponent. Kat closed the distance and began a rapid series of stabs and physical strikes. Sinera twirled her bow swiftly to block the daggers while meeting Kat's strikes with her own. Sinera blocked a kick that jarred her arms as she retaliated with slashes of her bow. Kat blocked before feinting right and scoring a jab in Sinera's face. Not wasting a second, Kat lunged forward for another strike, Sinera ducked, grabbed Kat's arm, and, using the momentum, hurled Kat away from her.

Kat landed flat on her back, the blow knocking the air out of her lungs. Before she could rise, an arrow was pointed at her face while Sinera kicked Kat's daggers away. Kat closed her eyes in defeat and waited for the blow. After a second, she opened them to see Sinera standing over her with a hand outstretched. Kat took it before being led to her father. Sinera strode over to her brother and began healing him, while Kat was avoiding eye contact with her father.

Yorou, however, looked pleased as he gave his daughter a gentle hug and whispered, "You did wonderfully. I'm proud of you, and your mother would be too."

Kat stiffened at that before returning the embrace. Sinera, Nyzir, and Sevastian approached, with Sinera looking slightly tired, Nyzir appearing the same, and Sevastian looking proud.

Yorou looked at them with a smile and then said, "You three did well. Now we will rest for an hour before splitting. Nyzir, I want you, your sister, and Kat here to go and hunt. This will be survival training and to see if you three can get along. Sevastian and I will do our own hunting as well."

He released Kat, who looked both worried and pleased. Nyzir kept a hand in front of his face as he moved through the hard wind, following Kat, with Sinera next to him. Kat was leading them to a series of caves she had discovered that apparently housed trolls.

When Nyzir questioned why they would hunt trolls, Kat looked incredulous before saying, "We need meat, Nyzir, and those monsters have killed plenty of us. It's kill or be killed up here. Besides, trolls don't taste too bad."

They found the caves several leagues from Iketh, nestled into a small mountain. Kat had warned them of the troll's sharp sense of smell and hearing but weak eyesight. They crept their way into the first cave. The smell punched Nyzir in the gut. An acrid smell of blood-soaked fur and old meat accompanied the growls and sounds of eating whatever the trolls had caught. Nyzir slowly peered inside, and the sight made his eyes widen. Two trolls sat in the cave. They towered over Nyzir even while sitting. He saw yellow teeth flecked with blood and ebony claws as long as Nyzir's hand. Their hides were the same color as the snow around them.

Kat pulled Nyzir back and whispered, "Our best strategy is to ambush them. Can you use your crystal to pin those two while I and Sinera finish them?"

Nyzir looked thoughtful before a grin swept up. "I'm on it," he replied before he crouched outside to get ready.

Nyzir placed a hand on the ground and concentrated. Though he had been taught to channel magic through his weapon as a medium, that method merely made it easier to use magic on the fly, excellent on the battlefield, but when allowed, Nyzir wanted to hone his skill. A sly smile graced his lips as his crystal erupted from the floor and walls of the cave. Taking the form of speared hooks, they punctured the trolls' feet and arms before sinking back into the ground, rooting them in place.

The trolls howled in agony and thrashed, trying to break free. Nyzir gritted his teeth. The trolls were strong. Nyzir gripped the rock hard as he struggled to keep the trolls chained. Sinera and Kat rushed into the cave and killed the trolls in sprays of scarlet. Nyzir released the crystal and entered the cave. The trolls' white fur was splattered with blood from either an opened throat or multiple stab wounds. They all drew their knives and set about skinning and carving out the meat. They packed the meat in sacks made of the trolls' flesh and wiped the gore off with snow before heading back.

The sun was beginning to wane when Nyzir, Sinera, and Kat had arrived at Iketh. When they entered their home, Nyzir saw Sevastian and Yorou storing meat before looking at them.

"Ah-ha! You made it back," Yorou exclaimed before giving his daughter a hug. He then inspected the meat and judged it a good hunt.

After they stored everything, a knock was heard. Yorou opened the door, and Prak entered, slightly leaning on his staff.

When seeing their surprised faces, Prak merely said, "Am I not allowed to see how our guests are doing?"

Yorou replied, "Of course, my friend. Your arrival was merely unexpected."

Prak nodded before approaching the mystic. Sevastian grasped Prak's hand firmly and said, "You shouldn't worry, Prak. We are doing fine. In fact, I think it's time we discussed Sinera's training."

Prak, however, looked confused. "I came to also see her training, so, Yorou, care to show us?"

Yorou looked between the two and then nodded. When they arrived at the training area, Yorou turned to Sinera. "You have already done some ice manipulation with helping my daughter make those chairs. Tell me, when you used the magic, did you feel clarity, as if you could think clearly?"

Sinera replied, "Yes, I did. Why?"

Yorou nodded. "We have a saying. 'We're as sharp as our ice, both in mind and in body.' When you use ice, it clears your mind of distraction, making you think more clearly." He grabbed his water skin and poured some into a bowl and then handed it to Sinera. "Your first task is to freeze the water without your weapon." Before Sinera could protest, Yorou rebutted, "You must be able to use magic without your weapon. It is merely an exercise in will. Go on. Show me your will."

Sinera looked at the water and envisioned it freezing, but nothing happened. She tried to find the feeling of cold clarity but couldn't feel it. She stared at the water before her. She knew ice was just frozen water, but what had Yorou meant by "will" being required? She stared at the water till it obscured her vision and focused her mind on freezing it. After a few long seconds, she felt it. The rush of a calming chill flooded her mind as the water froze completely.

Yorou looked impressed as he took the bowl and inspected the water. "That was well done for your first time. Don't get too excited. You have a long way to go and little time. I will be pushing you harder than you've been before. So tell me, do you have the will?"

Sinera looked Yorou in the eye before saying, "I do, Yorou. I'm ready for what you throw at me."

Yorou grinned, while Kat congratulated Sinera. Prak had a smile before heading to report to the other sages. Nyzir was smiling, proud of his sister. While Sevastian looked pleased, he also looked worried as he watched Kat and Sinera talking.

Nyzir spoke. "Master, are you all right?"

Sevastian looked at Nyzir. "I'm fine. Don't think I'll let you off easy. I'm still going to train you till you can't walk for a day, so prepare yourself."

Nyzir looked toward the setting sun, feeling its dying heat grace his body, and inhaled the wonderful chilly air. "Don't worry, Master. I'm ready."

CHAPTER 13

Nyzir gripped a strong rod of crystal as he steadied himself. He balanced on more rods from his perch a few yards under the tip of the mountain overlooking Iketh. Regaining his bearings, Nyzir inhaled the fresh cold mountain air. Somehow it always calmed him and made him loathe the thought of leaving. The view from the mountain was *breathtaking*, with Iketh and its people appearing as ants to the other mountains neighboring them.

Nyzir let a sigh escape before a grin swallowed it. They were leaving any day now. The training was long, hard, and worth it. Nyzir, Sinera, and even Kat had split their time between Sevastian and Yorou. They each could now, as Sevastian put it, "give a good workout" during a one-on-one sparring session. Nyzir and Sinera's magic training had produced some downright insidious applications.

Nyzir further trained in using the wind to affect the body. He continued to develop his ability to deprive air to his enemies. However, he discovered that when trying to use it on Sevastian, per his request, he had to first bypass the magic of his target as the magic resisted intrusion by fighting back, similar to how the magic fought off alcohol and poison. When Nyzir finally started to cease his master's air flow, Sevastian would merely hold his breath and incapacitate Nyzir, forcing him to release the air.

Sinera had, likewise, learned formidable uses of her elements. With Kat's help, she could make weapons out of her ice, though they were limited to quick bladed weapons, per her style. Her water healing had proven lifesaving during more vicious hunts and overzealous training as well as pretty dangerous when she used raw water as a concussive force.

Nyzir's grin stayed strong as, off in the distance, he saw the faint outline of Sinera and Kat returning from some "girl time," though Nyzir highly doubted they snuck off to play with dolls. Deciding to greet them, Nyzir let go of the crystal and leaned backward, allowing gravity to take hold. He shifted his fall so as not to land headfirst into the mountain. The wind whistled past him as a laugh erupted from his chest. Though Sevastian had often dubbed this "unnecessarily risky and foolish," Nyzir reveled in it. The feeling of freedom this gave was indescribable. As he saw the base of the mountain approaching rapidly, Nyzir summoned the wind to right himself, and he shot into the air. He allowed himself a few corkscrews before shooting toward his sister and friend. Below, he saw children and even adults looking up with both astonishment and bewilderment. Nyzir saw Kat whisper something to Sinera, who, in return, flashed a mischievous smirk before grabbing her bow and letting an arrow loose on her brother. The arrow flew at Nyzir swiftly, cutting through the faint clouds in between them. Nyzir used the wind to slow the arrow's ascent and, with a deft hand, plucked the arrow out of the sky. Nyzir descended swiftly, landing unsteadily as he stumbled. Nyzir mentally kicked himself. It would take more work to time the landing right. A gale of laughter snapped Nyzir's thoughts like a twig. Kat was holding her sides so as not to double over, while Sinera had a cheeky grin that wouldn't go away.

"Look here, Kat." Sinera nudged her friend. "I've brought down my elusive flying brother. Wonder what my prize is." She finished with an evil grin that belonged more on Kat than her.

Nyzir faked a grunt and chucked the arrow back at his sister. Sinera caught it easily and returned it to her quiver. Upon closer inspection, Nyzir made out the outlines of bruises and blood streaks adorning them, though he couldn't tell if the blood was theirs or not. Shrugging, Nyzir turned and led them through Iketh.

The civilians were looking at Nyzir with trepidation and awe over his flying. Nyzir, however, merely wore an ear-to-ear grin as he made his way to Kat's house. When they arrived, Nyzir saw Sevastian talking with Yorou and Prak and grabbing his broadsword.

They turned at the sound of the door opening, and Sevastian said, "Good. You're finally here. We have to get going back to Minraz. I suggest you say your goodbyes." With that, he went back to preparing.

Kat immediately pulled her father aside and whispered into his ear. Yorou looked shocked and then resigned as he gestured the mystics over.

Yorou said slowly, "My daughter wishes to go with you to Minraz. Apparently, she has grown fond of you three."

Kat, for a moment, looked embarrassed at her father's words before looking Sevastian in the eye and saying strongly, "What? I've grown to like you guys, all right? I want to help you with saving your home." She looked at Yorou before continuing. "You three have filled a hole in my heart since Mother died long ago. I want to see the places you tell me about." She took a shaky breath before addressing Yorou. "Dad, I know how you feel about Mother, but she would want you to move on. Find a woman who will make you happy."

Silent tears fell from Yorou's eyes as he embraced his daughter. When they separated, Kat stood close to Nyzir and gave him a knowing smile. Nyzir looked away with a tinge of red on his neck, while Sinera merely rolled her eyes. Kat's affection for her brother was almost funny. Adopting a sad smile, Prak approached them. As he stood before them, Sevastian appeared out of their room with a wary look about him. Prak spoke then, a sense of calm finality dripping from his words.

"Know that, though you leave us, you will always be welcome, should you desire sanctuary or assistance. Take comfort in knowing that our goddess is watching over you and that you have her blessing."

With that, he gave each of them a kiss on the brow, which resulted in a pleasant chill coursing through their bodies. Nyzir, Sinera, and Kat decided to follow Sevastian's example and began preparing to leave.

Two days of hard travel brought them through a forest that separated them from Minraz. Their unicorns had been left to graze as Sevastian led his students down a trail that cut through the forest. Sevastian paused when the sound of crunching leaves was heard ahead of them. He glanced at his students. Nyzir opened his mouth, but Sevastian hissed, "Quiet." Nyzir's mouth snapped shut.

Sevastian led them down the path when they saw a figure approaching. The figure was dressed in a nondescript dark cloak to protect him from the humid forest air. Kat, having the best eyes among them, subtly gestured to the person's hip. A handle was made barely visible by the cloak and the rays of sunlight darting through the trees. The person paused when he was within ten paces of the mystics. He threw his hood back, revealing greasy black hair that reached the man's shoulders. A narrow face, calculating gray eyes, and a wiry frame completed his build. The man gazed over the four of them, eyes lingering on their weapons.

"Greetings, friend," Sevastian said airily. "Don't mind us. We're just returning home from some traveling." While not a lie, it did cause the man's eyebrow's to rise.

The man spoke. "Traveling, you say?" His voice was hoarse, as though he hadn't used it in ages. His eyes were once again trained on their weapons. "You're well armed for being just travelers."

Sevastian flashed a smile that didn't reach his hardening eyes. "I could say the same about you," he rebutted.

The man grunted. "These are hard times. Got to have protection from the beasts out there." His eyes once again looked over them before lingering on Sevastian.

Sevastian, deciding enough was enough, asked, "Who are you?"

The man smiled before his hand eased its way to the hilt concealed in its cloak. "I'm surprised you don't recognize me," he said slowly. "After all, how could you forget your own brother?"

Sevastian's breath hitched, body tensing, before he uttered a single word. *"Williem?"*

Williem's laugh reminded Nyzir of glass shattering. "Did you forget about me so easily, brother? Well, I haven't forgotten what I owe you for the death you caused."

Sevastian looked at his brother with something akin to pity. "Is that why you stand before me, to kill me for something that wasn't my fault? Sara chose the mission. We had no right to govern her life."

"Bullshit. You knew the mission was out of her league yet still got Mom and Dad to stop me from going with our little sister!"

Sevastian let a sigh escape him. "Sara knew what she was getting into, and I respected her for that. That doesn't mean I don't feel your pain, but going after me won't bring our sister back."

After a few seconds, low chuckling was heard from Williem, building and building till the laugh rang across the trees. Birds squawked and flew away while the laugh died down. Recovering, Williem looked at Sevastian with a wild gleam in his eye.

"You're still so foolish. It's adorable, little brother. I haven't come to kill you. You allowed someone I cared for to die, and now I'm going to take something you hold dear."

Nyzir had to take a step back as waves of intense heat assailed him. Kat and Sinera were similarly affected by Sevastian's magic. Nyzir looked in shock as their master's body glowed a faint red. Only Williem seemed unfazed, though he too had a faint red outline surrounding him, which puzzled Nyzir. Did they both use heat? Sevastian looked at his students, and Nyzir felt a shudder take him. There was a look of such fury that Nyzir had never seen on their typical laid-back mentor.

In a calm voice that belayed his ferocity, Sevastian said, "Consider this a free lesson, you three. This is how I fight when I'm not holding back." Sevastian drew his broadsword and held it ready. "Also," he added, "don't interfere unless you deem it absolutely necessary. I don't want you guys caught in the crossfire."

For a second, Sevastian and Williem merely eyed each other like wolves trying to prove who the alpha was. Then, seemingly in sync, they met with a clash of steel and magic. Williem's blade was a single-edged sword as wide as two thumbs. Though it was thin, it held its own against Sevastian's broadsword. Nyzir watched in awe as the brothers fought with a skill that he had never seen. Throughout their numerous spars, Nyzir would marvel at the ease in which Sevastian wielded his heavy weapon. Now, however, Sevastian's arms were a blur of motion as they clashed with Williem's equally fast swordplay.

After a few seconds, they broke their dance to breathe, both eyeing the other before encasing their swords with their magic. Kat looked intrigued as molten rock formed on Williem's sword. Nyzir's eyes widened. Williem, it seemed, used magma, the sub element of heat. This time, Sevastian and Williem's blows were punctuated with sparks as the elements seemed to be trying to overpower each other.

Sinera watched the battle critically. Her mentor and his brother seemed dead even as swordsmen, and their magic wasn't helping. Glancing at her brother, she could tell he came to the same conclusion by him gripping his halberd. Nyzir and Sinera both nodded to each other. They were going to have to help.

Nyzir stabbed the butt of his halberd into the earth and sent crystal snaking through the soil before it erupted from the ground, its tip aiming for Williem's side. But William jumped on the crystal and leapt onto a low-hanging branch. Nyzir launched himself into the air and, keeping himself afloat with the wind, struck at Williem with Tempest. Williem effortlessly blocked his strikes while returning his own. Suddenly, Williem's hand twitched, and Nyzir felt searing pain in his legs. Looking down, he saw hardening magma attaching to them. With a wild laugh, Williem kicked Nyzir back to earth. Only a desperate blanket of wind saved Nyzir from a broken spine. It still hurt though.

Williem landed on the ground with a roll before lunging at Nyzir, sword poised for his chest. Before the blade made contact, an arrow made out of ice connected with the sword. Nyzir threw his arm in front of his face, knowing what would happen as the arrowhead exploded in frozen shrapnel. Shards pierced Nyzir's arm, but he knew they were nothing compared to the scream that tore the air. Moving his arm, Nyzir stared in shock. Blood leaked from several wounds in Williem's face, but what shocked him was the shard that had lodged in Williem's right eye.

Sevastian dashed forward and landed a kick on his brother that sent him on his back before grabbing Nyzir and dragging him back to his sister and Kat. With a curse, Sevastian sliced the magma that was attached to Nyzir, and Sinera went about trying to heal him. Kat stood beside Sevastian as they watched his brother rise. Kat looked disgusted as Williem placed a hand over his eye and carefully pulled out the shard. Blood pooled out of Williem's eye as he struggled to stem the flow. Gazing at his brother with hate and pain, Williem retreated into the woods. Kat started to go after him, but Sevastian stopped her.

With a resigned expression on his face, Sevastian said, "Let him go lick his wounds. We have to get to Minraz." There was sadness but also resignation in his voice as he checked on Nyzir's legs.

While not fully healed, Nyzir assured them he could walk. Gingerly, they saddled up and exited the forest at full gallop.

In the distance, they saw Minraz. Some parts of the city were on fire, and swarming it were all manner of monsters, ranging from chimeras to goblins, even trolls, and in the sky—Nyzir paled—were a pack of griffins. Sevastian, sensing Nyzir's unease, gave him a reassuring nod. Kat was gazing at Minraz with a mixture of awe and horror. She had never seen these creatures before but knew that there was one thing that never changed—everything was killable.

Sevastian looked at his students before saying with a confidence Nyzir could tell was slightly forced, "What are we waiting for? Let's drive these beasts from our home."

CHAPTER 14

The scent of blood, both human and beast, caused the hairs on Nyzir's neck to stand erect and caused the unicorns to go into hysterics. Realizing the unicorns could do little for them, Sevastian had them dismount and rush through the craggy hole that had once been the main entrance to Minraz. Upon entering the city, they staggered back as the amount of magic in the air was palpable. In Nyzir's mind, comparing this to the battle between Sevastian and Williem was comparing a gale to a light breeze. Nyzir heard a shriek above and saw the griffins flying above, searching for prey. With the mystics fighting to repel the monsters in the streets, they could not focus on the griffins.

Nyzir turned to his mentor and said, "Master, you should take Kat and Sinera and help slow down these guys." He once again looked up and swallowed. "I'll handle the griffins."

Sevastian looked torn. While he had no doubt of Nyzir's skill, taking on several griffins would not be easy, but he knew he had no choice. With a deep breath, he said, "Fine. Just make sure you come back, and I don't need you or Sinera to refer to me as Master. Consider this battle your final test to see if your worthy of being mystics." With that, he led Kat and Sinera down a side street, cutting up goblins foolish enough to attack.

Nyzir stabbed his halberd into the ground and covered it in crystal. *This is all I've got. Better use it right*, he thought before launching himself into the blue-and-white sky above.

Nyzir moved swiftly through the air as he maneuvered to reach his target, a griffin that looked a little younger and smaller than the others. Its brown feathers were more of a pale tan rather than the color of oak. Nyzir flew around the griffin and, before it could react, impaled a hand-sized crystal into the beast's neck at the back. Concentrating, Nyzir shaped the crystal inside the griffin's bloodstream to hook onto the inside of its neck. Nyzir landed a bit hard on the creature's back and grabbed his makeshift handle while drawing his halberd. The griffin shook and bucked as it tried to dislodge Nyzir, but he held on while fending off another griffin. With a desperate swipe, Nyzir severed several nerves in the beast's wing, rendering it all but useless. With a furious shriek, the clipped griffin bit at Nyzir, but he dodged and rammed the tip of his halberd up the beast's chin.

Nyzir withdrew the halberd, twisted it in two, and, after focusing, hurled the bottom end into the face of another of the monsters. This one dropped like a stone, and Nyzir dived off his mount to race the dead griffin to the street floor. Using the wind to increase momentum, Nyzir grabbed his makeshift spear, ripped it out, then twisted his body, and desperately hurled it at one of the three remaining monsters. It stabbed a griffin in the underbelly and stayed lodged in.

Nyzir flew back to the youngest griffin. While dodging its claws and beak, he didn't register the clubbed tail that slammed into the side of his head. Stars exploded behind Nyzir's eyes as he grabbed at the handle he had made. With the griffin's flapping and constant twisting, Nyzir feared his arm would either dislocate or be ripped off. Grunting with pain, Nyzir forced himself onto the monsters back before making a throwing knife out of crystal. While not as skilled as his sister, Nyzir knew his accuracy was adequate for this. He hurled the throwing knife in a dizzying arc at the griffin advancing on him. It landed in its opened beak. Quickly, Nyzir willed the crystal to expand inside the griffin's maw. The crystal grew and impaled the monster in the brain.

As the now dead beast lost life in its body, it was still moving toward Nyzir. Before he could move, the body slammed into the griffin he was riding, throwing them to the side. As they tumbled, Nyzir was dislodged from his unwilling mount, and it clawed at him with razor-sharp talons. Nyzir screamed as he received deep slashes across his chest, blood immediately seeping from the wounds. Nyzir, feeling already fatigued from the battle, knew he had to act quickly.

He grabbed a handful of crystal and put it to his chest. At his will, the crystal grew to cover the wound, though only just. Still in pain, Nyzir stabbed the griffin in the neck—hard. The beast cried out in pain as its eyes rolled back, while Nyzir released his grip on it, using the wind to keep him aloft. Knowing timing was crucial, Nyzir gazed at the final griffin, spear still impaled in its belly. With an angry shriek, it dove at Nyzir. Nyzir drew Tempest and summoned the wind around him to encase his blade. The monster was atop him in an instant, stabbing and pecking. Nyzir dodged just in time and slashed at its neck. The blade passed through the griffin like a knife cutting through bread, and with a savage yank, Nyzir severed the beast's head.

Blood splattered onto Nyzir's face and torso, filling his nose with the awful stench and his mouth with the taste of metal. Nyzir sheathed Tempest and grabbed the other end of his halberd, letting the griffin pull him to earth. As the ground rapidly approached, Nyzir grabbed the dead griffin and surrounded as much of his body in crystal as he could. All Nyzir could do was wait for the impact.

Sevastian led Sinera and Kat down an alleyway that connected two roads. He weaved through forgotten trash and bloodied corpses before stopping at the entryway. Footsteps were heard, and Sevastian saw a Forsworn leaning against an abandoned cart. The man was covered in gore, and a good chunk of his face looked roasted. Yet even with the injuries, his pale eyes found them. The man staggered to his feet, leaning on a broken stick as he hobbled over.

Sinera was about to run out to help the man, but Sevastian grabbed her shoulder forcefully. A split second later, a whistling sound was heard. Before Sinera could open her mouth, a large boulder smashed into the Forsworn, sending him flying with the sound of crunching bone. Sinera stared in horror before they felt the ground shake underneath them. Then she felt the grunts and snarls of something large reverberate in her bones.

A shadow loomed over them as a cyclops overshadowed the sunlight. Its gray hide was leathery, but the shadows made it look black. A loincloth made of some animal covered its waist. In its hand was a crude wooden club. Its single beady red eye swiveled in the alley, while its snout breathed in large amounts of air. Sevastian subtly gestured for Sinera and Kat to freeze. Cyclopses had poor daylight eyesight, being nocturnal by nature, but compensated with a good sense of smell.

Sevastian thanked whatever deities existed for their location as the smell of dead bodies and garbage would mask their scent. The cyclops gave a grunt before moving in the direction of the thrown boulder. They heard the boulder being lifted, and the unmistakable sound of chewing ensued. Kat looked disgusted before Sevastian raised his hand. He gestured to where the cyclops went and then tightly closed his fist. Kat and Sinera nodded before following Sevastian and readying their weapons.

Sevastian crept after the cyclops, using the shadows of the buildings to stay hidden. He was forced to watch his footing on the slick cobblestones. Sinera and Kat remained a little behind, ready to strike. Sevastian readied his blade while eyeing the cyclops's legs. With its legs being so thick, he would need to be precise. Seeing his target, Sevastian set his sword ablaze with heat before stabbing it into the back of the cyclops's knee.

The cyclops snarled in pain as it dropped to one knee before swiping at its attacker. Sevastian dodged back, with the broadsword still embedded in the cyclops. Kat and Sinera dashed past Sevastian, weapons ready. Kat used the cyclops's leg as leverage to hoist herself up the monster's broad back. The monster flailed its arms in an attempt to knock her off, but Kat was too quick. She got on the cyclops's shoulders and stabbed her daggers deep into its ears. Sinera rolled in between the cyclops's legs, and as it howled in agony, she released an arrow into its open maw. The cyclops's roar was cut short as it descended to the ground like a marionette with its strings severed. As it crashed to earth, Kat jumped off and landed slightly off balance before punching the air.

"Ha!" Kat laughed. "We kicked this monster's arse."

She had a wild look in her eye that caused Sinera to shake her head and smile. One thing she had learned quickly about Kat was that she enjoyed a good fight and reveled in each victory. Sevastian grabbed his sword before scraping the blood off with the cyclops's loincloth.

Heavy footsteps were heard, causing Sevastian, Kat, and Sinera to prepare for another fight, only for Carter to appear. His armor was torn and covered in blood as if he had been in the thickest of the fighting, which, given his status, was probably true. He had a multitude of wounds on his person, though they looked shallow. His mace was rusted red and dripping blood, while his shield was ripped in half. The hollow look in his sun-colored eyes turned to surprise and then downright joy in a heartbeat upon seeing Sinera. In an instant, he was embracing his daughter, heedless of his bloodied state. Sinera returned the gesture. Carter stepped back and appraised his daughter.

"It's wonderful to see you again, Sinera." Carter spoke softly while gripping Sinera's shoulders as though she might disappear. "Where's Nyzir?" Carter asked, noticing his absence.

Sevastian stepped forward then, his face a careful construct of neutrality as he spoke. "Nyzir's battling the griffins in the sky. He told us he would be fine and to figure out what's going on."

Carter looked shocked by the proclamation, but then he glared. "And why didn't you support him? Did you forget you're also supposed to help my children as well as train them?"

Sevastian kept his neutral composure, save for a tightening of his jaw. It hurt him just as much as Carter. "I trust my apprentice," he said to Carter. "Do you not trust your son?"

Carter's eyes widened in shock before a resigned look swept his features and the tension drained from him.   In a controlled voice, Carter replied, "I trust my family. I've had to accept that I can't protect them from every danger. That doesn't mean I want to know my son is in danger and be reminded that I'm powerless to help."

Sevastian gave a small smile before grasping Carter's arm. Looking his superior dead in the eye, Sevastian said, "I know it's hard, but Nyzir can look after himself. Believe it or not, he's one tough guy to keep down. I should know."

A small chuckle escaped Carter as he too grasped Sevastian's arm. "I know, and I'm grateful." His gaze finally settled on Kat, who had heard several stories about him from Nyzir and Sinera.

Kat, deciding to get straight at it, thrust her hand at Carter. "M'name's Kat," she said briskly.

Carter's eyes gleamed as he shook her hand before a laugh escaped him. Kat's eyes widened before Carter spoke. "You've got attitude. That's what I like to see." He finished with a chuckle before gesturing them to follow.

Sevastian spoke as they moved carefully through the tarnished street. "Carter, what's the situation? Why have we not seen any live mystics?" He decided against mentioning the one they had avenged.

Carter's eyes darkened as he clenched his mace tightly. "These beasts were either more cunning than we expected or have something pulling their strings." Carter spoke tiredly. "We were prepared thanks to your letter, so we held them for a while. Then more of them appeared and at different areas of the city. We had to spread our forces even more than they already were." As he spoke, he crushed the skull of a twitching goblin without a second glance. "We were forced to retreat, cutting off side streets and blocking as many alleys as we could. Then we were informed the empress had a plan and would need us to defend her tower. We've been doing that for the better part of an hour now." He stopped to close the eyes of a dead Forsworn while whispering a prayer. Straightening, he continued. "I was then ordered to check some of the closed-off areas for survivors, and that's how I found you." He finished with a deep breath.

That little explanation had seemingly drained the Forsworn captain. Sevastian offered him his water skin, and Carter drank deeply before handing it back. Looking a little refreshed, Carter led Sevastian, Kat, and Sinera along more alleyways and deserted streets. All the while, they hoped to see Nyzir when they arrived.

CHAPTER 15

The first thing Nyzir felt when he regained consciousness was the feeling that the inside of his body was on fire. While he was no stranger to injury, it felt like his insides were melting. Even trying to move an inch caused torrents of agony. Upon inhaling, he coughed up a glob of blood.

A soft voice spoke then. "Really, Nyzir? Even after you leave my teachings, your still cause trouble?"

Nyzir's eyes struggled to open, only for the light to force them shut again. Baring his teeth at the pain, Nyzir forced his eyes open. Crouching before him was Lori, wearing a bloody Forsworn uniform. In her hand was a blood-slicked scimitar, while her other hand hovered over Nyzir. His eyes widened as water slowly congealed on him and set about healing him. Though it was painful, Nyzir called a smile to his face.

"Thought you were retired, Lori," he said to her.

Lori looked at Nyzir with a scowl before replying, "Just because I'm retired doesn't mean I won't defend my home, and you'd better watch your stunts. I'm not as skilled in healing as I was." Her face turned slightly pale as she finished speaking.

Nyzir merely kept his grin on. "But, Lori, you know I respond better with action rather than your boring lectures," Nyzir teased.

Lori merely sighed as she allowed the water to be absorbed into Nyzir. Lori leaned back and looked around, causing Nyzir to slowly lift his head and assess his surroundings. He was lying on the broken wing of one of the griffins he had killed. The other four were scattered about, their bodies broken by the impact. Nyzir's eyes widened, and he was unsure if what he saw was real. He had managed to kill the five griffins. Lori looked down at Nyzir before offering him a hand and a smile. Nyzir grasped it and allowed her to pull him to his feet. Immediately, Nyzir realized his right leg must have broken as it refused to support him, leaving him to lean heavily on Lori.

Lori bore a look of worry as she led Nyzir to one of the griffins, which had his halberd stuck in it. Grimacing, Nyzir withdrew his weapon and stuck it into the ground, allowing it to bear some of his weight. Nyzir tried to walk, only to almost lose his balance if not for Lori catching him. Nyzir was appalled at how weak he felt. It was as if his body had been sucked of energy. Snarling past gritted teeth, Nyzir forced himself upright, only for Lori to grab his arm and sling it around her shoulder.

Giving his former teacher a thankful look, he allowed her to lead him down the streets through Minraz. She asked him what had happened during his training, which made Nyzir smile as he gave her a shortened version of his, Sinera, and Sevastian's adventure. Lori was impressed with Nyzir's and Sinera's accomplishments as well as teasing him about Kat, much to his frustration.

Nyzir's ears perked as he heard the sound of metal sliding through flesh, accompanied by a throaty scream. He looked at Lori curiously.

"Think we have company?" he asked, gripping his halberd tightly.

"Let's see if it's good or bad first," Lori replied as she helped Nyzir through an abandoned house that linked the two streets.

The house itself was in poor condition. If the drying blood and pulverized bodies were any indication, a brutal fight had taken place. Lori and Nyzir navigated the house carefully before leaving through the back door. What greeted them was a rolling goblin head, green blood leaving a trail as it rolled along. Nyzir turned, only to be greeted by Sinera, Kat, Sevastian, and, strangely enough, Carter.

Kat and Sinera immediately relieved Lori of Nyzir. Lori threw her arms around Sevastian, who accepted the hug graciously before prying her off gently. Carter, meanwhile, caught Nyzir in a rough embrace, only for Nyzir's hiss of pain to cause him to back off. Carter looked over his son worriedly. Nyzir's shirt and coat had talon marks on them, exposing partially healed claw wounds. His leg was at a slightly altered angle, forcing him to grip Sinera to stand, but Carter knew it could have been a hell of a lot worse.

Gently ruffling Nyzir's hair, much to his son's chagrin, Carter spoke gently. "Am I right in thinking that you're being here means you killed those griffins you foolishly chose to take on alone?" His sun-colored eyes bored into Nyzir's equally yellow hues.

Nyzir kept the stare as long as he could before averting his eyes. In a slightly shaky voice, Nyzir replied, "Yes, Father."

Carter's hand grasped his son's shoulder to the point of causing pain, forcing him to meet Carter's gaze. What he saw sent a chill down his spine. The shadows of tears gleamed in the corners of Carter's eyes before slowly trailing down his down his face. Carter spoke with a tenderness Nyzir hadn't heard since he and Sinera were kids, when Carter would tell them how he looked forward to seeing his children succeed.

"Nyzir," Carter began, "I understand that you and Sinera have grown much in your time away, and though it pains me, I must accept that I can't protect you two from the horrors of the world. However, I can ask one thing. Don't do anything as reckless as what you did without thinking of others. Can you imagine what I, Helena, or Sinera would think if you died?"

Nyzir looked downcast before Carter placed a kiss on his forehead. Carter continued, "That being said, know that I am proud of you, son, as you should be too."

A smile ghosted across Carter's face before he stiffened, his posture becoming alert. After a second, Nyzir heard it too—a kind of throaty purr mixed with a growl as something fluttered in the breeze. The whistle of something cutting through the air was heard as a black stinger arched across the building in front of them and stabbed for Nyzir and Carter.

Before the stinger struck, Sevastian got between them and intercepted it with his broadsword. The stinger tried to get around, but Sevastian angled it away before slashing at it. However, the stinger withdrew quickly behind the building. Nyzir began to follow the tail, but his father stopped him. Carter watched the buildings in front of him warily, straining his ears for any sound. The purring was replaced by an agitated growl that caused Nyzir to shiver a bit.

Suddenly, the sound of something digging into the ground was heard. Then a gust of wind swept at them as something large launched over the building. In an instant, Carter drew his mace, and the earth around them rose to encase them in a dome. A heavy impact slammed into the dome, causing it to develop cracks, and forced Carter to take a step back as he strained to keep whatever creature this was at bay. The sound of stomping was heard and caused the cracks to multiply, forcing Carter to put a hand to the dome in an attempt to seal the cracks, which only partially succeeded.

In a stern voice, Carter spoke. "When I say so, get away from me as fast as you can."

Nyzir was shocked by the order, but Sevastian's glare stopped him from questioning his father.

Carter smiled grimly before shouting, "Now!"

As the word escaped him, Carter let the dome break. Sevastian forced his way through the weakening earth and, grabbing Nyzir by the waist, hurled him clear of the monster. Nyzir rolled with the impact and landed several yards away. When Nyzir looked up, he saw what had attacked them. Large bat-like wings were folded at the creature's sides. Its feline body was a mass of gold fur, while its face was contorted into a monster version of a contemptible sneer as it surveyed its latest meal. Its stinger tail swayed slowly, as if watching them.

Nyzir looked in shock as the manticore reared back to avoid Carter's mace before swatting at him as though he were a fly. Carter was able to block the paw with his shield, but he was still sent flying by the collision. Sevastian and Sinera moved to back up Carter. Kat ran to Nyzir and set about getting him to lie against one of the buildings, away from the fight. When Nyzir was secure, Kat drew her daggers. Nyzir opened his mouth, but Kat placed a finger on his lips to silence him.

In an almost tender voice, she whispered. "Nyzir, don' worry 'bout me. Y'know I can look after m'self." Seeing the pained look in his eyes caused Kat to sigh. "Look," Kat said, "you're in no condition to fight, alrigh'? You sit this one out, and we'll take care of him." She flashed Nyzir a broad grin, which made the back of his neck flush, and then she ran over to the battle.

Nyzir watched, fascinated, as Kat moved with the elegance of a dancer as she wove her way past sharp claws to perform swift stabs and cuts at the manticore. However, the strikes seemed only to irritate it as it continued to try and kill them. Carter and Sevastian were doing a good job at keeping the manticore distracted while Sinera and Kat tried to bring it down. Sinera rolled under the manticore and began slashing at it with her bow and dagger. Kat jumped on top of the manticore and tried to get at its head. Hot blood splashed onto Sinera from the deep slashes she had left in the manticore's belly before she got out from under it to avoid being stomped on. Kat swiftly clambered up the monster's furry back until she reached its head, and then she began stabbing at the manticore's face and eyes.

The manticore growled and began shaking itself violently as if getting water off. While Kat held on for a few seconds, her fingers started to lose their grip just as the manticore threw its head back. Head met chest as Kat was thrown back by the force of the headbutt, landing with a crunch against the cobblestone streets. Sevastian dodged a swipe before stabbing rapidly at the manticore's nose. The manticore reared its head back as blood and pus dribbled down its snout and into its bared jaws. The manticore twisted its head as arrows punctured its wings, courtesy of Sinera. By now, the manticore was getting frustrated by the annoyance of these three. Peripherally, the manticore saw Nyzir and Kat, clearly unable to move. With a snarl of triumph, the manticore bounded toward them, with Carter hot on its heels.

Nyzir saw the monster approaching quickly and tried to stand, only for his broken leg to give out and for him to release a silent scream of frustration. Nyzir saw Kat struggling to rise. Blood dripped from a wound on her head. She gripped her chest as her face contorted in pain. When she saw Nyzir looking at her, she grimaced before giving him a pained smile. Nyzir heard a triumphant growl and turned to see the manticore a few yards from them, where it launched itself at Kat while its tail stabbed at Nyzir. Nyzir stared as Kat's eyes widened in shock before she screamed in defiance at impending death, which caused Nyzir to smile to himself. Kat's determination was one of his favorite aspects of her, and he would be damned if he couldn't help her when she needed it.

Nyzir's eyes found Kat's, and he mouthed, "I'm sorry," before grabbing at his remaining power. Nyzir thrust his hand forward, and a small blast of wind struck Kat with the force of a sledgehammer. Kat went flying to the other side of the street. The manticore's claws slashed at air. Nyzir felt a brief rush of relief before he saw that the stinger was right on top of him. *Well*, Nyzir thought wryly, *at least I could save a friend in her time of need.* Nyzir stared at the tail approaching, a content smile on his face.

A flash of green intercepted his vision, and Nyzir gasped as Carter leapt in front of him as the tail found its mark. The sound of bone piercing through armor and flesh was acute to Nyzir. He heard his father gasp in pain as the venom entered him. However, to Nyzir's shock, Carter raised his mace and, with a cry of triumph, brought it down as hard as he could on the tail. Nyzir could see what appeared to be blades of earth on the mace as Carter struck again, partially tearing the stinger off. With an angry scream, the manticore lashed its tail out, attempting to throw Carter off, but Carter wasn't having it. He smashed the tail one more time. As the manticore flung him away, Carter took the stinger with him. Nyzir watched in horror as Carter was thrown through the air, only to land on a bed of water.

Nyzir saw his sister slowly level their father to earth before she stood and faced the manticore. Nyzir recoiled slightly at the look of pure hatred on his sister's face as she approached the manticore. Sinera glanced at her brother, her eyes saying one thing—"Do not interfere. He is mine." Nyzir could only nod hesitantly as Sinera twirled her bow before pointing it at the manticore.

At first, nothing happened, and then Sinera suddenly barked, "Die, you bastard!"

Then Nyzir noticed a churning in the manticore. It hunched over, clearly in pain, as it glared at Sinera, who merely glared back. The manticore's eyes bulged as water spewed from its mouth, only to encase its jaws and snout. Nyzir watched in horror as the manticore began thrashing about as it tried to get itself free. It attempted to spread its wings, only for hooks of water to spring from the ground and tear through the wings, pulling them to the ground. The manticore shook its head but to no avail. Its eyes rolled back in its head as it slumped to the ground, dead.

Sinera took several deep breaths before she strode purposefully to Nyzir. Nyzir looked at his sister with a small amount of fear. What he had seen her do to the manticore truly unnerved him. Sinera grabbed Nyzir and hauled him to his feet before embracing him roughly. Nyzir felt Sinera shaking slightly as sobs racked her. He slowly returned the embrace and felt Sinera tighten her hold on him.

"I thought I was going to lose you," Nyzir heard her whisper.

He tentatively rubbed her back before she released him. Sinera gripped his arm and led him over to their father. Nyzir saw Kat staggering toward them, a makeshift bind wrapped around her head to stop the blood flow. Sevastian and Lori trailed behind her, with Lori looking impressed by Sinera's display. Sevastian face was unreadable.

Sinera, Nyzir, and Kat got to Carter's side quickly before carefully carrying him to lean against the wall of an abandoned bakery. Carter appeared to be struggling to keep his eyes focused before they settled on the three of them. A small smile graced his blood-caked face as he looked them over. He reached out and ruffled Nyzir's hair with a bloody palm.

"I'm so proud of you, Nyzir, and you, Sinera," Carter said softly before coughing up a glob of blood. "You've become skilled warriors, just like I knew you would." Carter took a shuddering breath before continuing. "I'm not going to be surviving this, so I won't ramble. I want you to look after your mother. Helena meant the world to me, so tell her I died defending our children. She deserves to know that much."

Carter's eyes bore into his children before they flicked over to Kat. The smile on his face grew slightly as he spoke to her. "Kat, I can see clearly that you care for my children, and they care for you. I want you to promise me that you will do all in your power to protect them since I can't anymore."

Kat looked startled by the request, but at a supportive nod from Nyzir, she replied slowly, "Don' worry. I have their backs, Captain."

Carter laughed so hard, it hurt. Wiping away streaks of blood from his mouth, he grinned at Kat. "I thought I told you to call me Carter. You're not under my command. Thank you. If we meet on the other side, let's share a drink and trade war stories, you hear?"

Kat smiled and replied, "I'm already lookin' forward to it."

Carter spoke then, addressing all three of them. "One last request. When you find the monsters that caused this suffering to our home, give 'em hell from me." Carter closed his eyes. His body shuddered slightly and lay still.

Nyzir felt tears in his eyes, but he wiped them away. There would be time for grieving once this was over. He felt Kat grab his arm and help him up. Sevastian and Lori approached then, both bearing expressions of sorrow as Sevastian knelt down and grabbed the stinger still impaled in Carter's stomach. Sevastian pulled it out and placed a red hot hand to the hole. After a second, Sevastian removed his hand, revealing a cauterized patch of flesh where the wound had been. Sevastian reached up and closed Carter's dead eyes before standing.

"It's the least I can do for him," Sevastian said calmly, though there was an undertone of grief in his voice.

Lori looked downcast but ready to push on. Kat and Sinera helped Nyzir move as they made a final push to the empress's tower. Stepping past the fallen mystics that littered the cobblestones, they turned onto a main street and saw their destination. The empress's tower had been fortified by a barricade of earth that encircled the tower, with both crystal and earth spikes protruding from it. Attempting to ram through it was a horde of monsters. As Nyzir watched, two trolls came barreling past where they were, charging toward the tower with murderous intent.

Nyzir then noticed several arrow slits in the barricade, and as if on cue, a multitude of arrows were launched at the trolls. The arrows punctured the trolls' legs and peppered their faces. The trolls only pushed harder, slamming into the barricade with a mindless determination that bordered on suicide. The spikes tore through their flesh easily as the trolls flailed and tried to reach over and grab the occupants. Several spear tips were thrust upward and impaled the groping arms, forcing them to go limp. After a few seconds, the trolls succumbed to blood loss and sagged like sacks of potatoes.

Before Nyzir could feel any exhilaration for this minor victory, he heard a roar that crashed into him like a waterfall, forcing him to cover his ears. He was vaguely aware of the others doing the same. Nyzir felt a shadow pass overhead and looked up, only to see the dragon that had spoken to them those months ago. With each flap of its heavy wings, the air vibrated and crashed around them. The dragon's red eyes were filled with malice as it eyed the tower as if it were a steak dinner. Nyzir could only watch in horror. If this was the child angry, Nyzir was worried what would happen if his sire were to return. A faint red crawled its way up the dragon's throat as it opened its maw.

Nyzir felt Sevastian grip his shoulder and whisper, "Do you feel that, from the tower?"

Nyzir could only stare in confusion before he felt the magic being gathered at the tower. If Nyzir could describe it, it felt like a giant heartbeat with magic pulsing in the air. Suddenly, with a sound that resembled the chime of a bell, a pillar of iridescent yellow light bloomed forth to wrap and encase the tower. Before Nyzir blinked, the light pushed itself outward, passing over the barricade and pushing the trolls away. After a second, the strange light passed over Nyzir. It felt like he had been given a warm hug. Nyzir watched the dragon snarl and send a stream of fire at the light, only for it to dissipate upon contact. After a few seconds, the light had encased the entirety of Minraz in a pale yellow dome. The dragon released a scream of frustration as it battered at the dome with powerful strikes from its claws and tail, only for them to leave no mark.

The dragon spoke then, its voice gripped by cold fury. *Very clever, humans. You may have survived for now, but I won't be leaving without a little compensation.*

The dragon inhaled sharply, and Nyzir saw something transparent float toward the dragon, only to be stopped by the dome. The dragon gnashed its teeth and inhaled more strongly. The substance seemed to slide through the dome as if it were mud, only to be sucked into the dragon. The dragon continued for a few seconds before it released a strangled breath, staring at the dome in anger. Nyzir heard the sound of earth shattering and turned to see the barricade destroyed.

Out of the rubble stepped Empress Sylia, leaning on a Forsworn for support. Nyzir's breath was caught in his throat. Sylia looked to have aged a decade since he had last seen her. Sylia's face bore fragile lines proudly. Her silver hair was streaked with white, and her gait had a slight limp, but her emerald eyes shone as she glared at the dragon.

In a strong voice that cemented her authority, she addressed the dragon. "I will *not* allow you to further desecrate our city. You have no power here!"

The dragon stared at Sylia, and she stared back before the dragon, with a contemptuous sniff, turned away.

Your time will come, humans, and I will await it eagerly. The dragon then flared its wings and took off.

Sylia sagged, gripping the Forsworn tightly to remain upright. Sevastian stepped out of the corner, with Lori close behind, while Kat and Sinera struggled to support Nyzir's weight. Sylia turned, and her eyes widened as she saw them. Tears sprung in her eyes as she allowed the Forsworn to help her toward them. Now that the barricade was down, Nyzir caught a glimpse of several dozens of exhausted Forsworn and mystics. When Sylia reached them, she wrapped Nyzir and Sinera in a tight embrace while her tears stained their clothes. They returned the embrace, even through Nyzir's hiss of pain. When Sylia pulled back, she had a look of happiness on her face that rivaled the sun.

She spoke then, quick and softly. "I understand you must have questions, and I will be more than happy to answer them, but first, we need to get our wounded healed and our people back home. Is that understood?"

Nyzir and Sinera nodded before Sylia led them to her tower, already ordering those injured to accompany them. Nyzir felt relief. Their home was safe if scared, but that could be mended. What clutched at Nyzir's heart like a vice was what he was going to say to his mother about Carter's death.

Chapter 16

The pale yellow rays of the rising sun stabbed at Nyzir's eyelids, forcing them open. Nyzir was greeted by the now familiar white ceiling of the infirmary. A groan escaped Nyzir. Even though this was only his third day, it already felt like torture to him. Sitting up slowly, he moved his mended leg experimentally. While there was still slight discomfort, Nyzir felt he could move freely again. Glancing downward, he saw that the bandages on his chest were gone, revealing faint but noticeable scars, which didn't bother him, for they proved what he could accomplish.

Sadness still lingered in his heart from the day before, when he had explained to his mother about Carter's death. The reaction had been as he had expected, with his mother crying for a good ten minutes while Nyzir and Sinera tried to comfort her.

In the end, Helena had embraced her children tightly and whispered, "At least I know you two are safe and that C-Carter didn't die for nothing." She hiccupped at Carter's name but otherwise merely held her children like a lifeline.

Nyzir jumped as footsteps were heard entering the infirmary. Glancing up, he saw Sinera and Sevastian approaching. Sevastian bore a grim look, and Sinera seemed to be forcing a smile. When they reached his bed, Sevastian placed Nyzir's folded clothes on his bed, while Sinera leaned her brother's weapons against his bed.

Sevastian looked Nyzir dead on and said in an emotionless voice, "It's time."

Nyzir felt what happiness he had drain into the bed under him. He had almost forgotten about the funeral. While he didn't know how many had died in the battle, he understood it had been a substantial amount. Nyzir sat up and grabbed his clothes before pulling a curtain around his bed for privacy. Breathing slowly, he set about dressing himself. A hiss escaped him when he ran his shirt over his healing chest, but otherwise, he felt little discomfort.

When he was clothed, Nyzir allowed a small smile to grace him. For some reason, Nyzir felt a strange comfort being in familiar clothes. He drew back the curtain and set about arming himself. With the familiar weight of Tempest and his halberd, Nyzir felt more complete than he had over the days in the infirmary. Sevastian and Sinera waited at the door for Nyzir to join them.

As they stepped out, Nyzir made sure to savor the heat and welcoming breeze. The sun painted Minraz in a multitude of oranges and yellows sliced through with red. Nyzir looked about him with a sadness he felt deep inside. Civilians and mystics alike were running to and fro, delivering messages about who needed what for repairs, with mystics trying to direct the strange anarchy while providing what assistance they could. As Nyzir moved among them, several civilians and mystics parted to let him pass. Nyzir felt sad eyes on him from the mystics and awed ones from the civilians. When Nyzir was about to speak, he saw two people approaching, both civilians in their early thirties. The man, whom Nyzir didn't recognize, spoke first.

"Young mystic"—he bowed slightly—"I know my wife and I speak for all around us when I say how grateful we are for what you did during our city's time of need."

As Nyzir was about to point out that he wasn't a mystic yet and ask what the man was talking about, he was interrupted by the man's wife.

"Do not attempt to downplay your achievements for the purpose of modesty." She spoke with a firmness that surprised Nyzir. "Those griffins would have caused large amounts of destruction and death to our city and guardians." She spared a glance at the mystics around them before leveling a piercing gaze on Nyzir. "Just know, young man, that we are all in debt to you and the brave mystics who defended our city." She smiled and led her husband back to the crowd.

Nyzir's eyes were wide as he ran what the woman had said in his head. While he was flattered that they spoke highly of him, he didn't know how to handle it. He felt someone grasp his hand, and he saw Sinera leading him through the mass of people toward the empress's tower. When they arrived, Nyzir saw Empress Sylia and Kat waiting for them. Nyzir was surprised to see Sylia leaning on a ceremonial staff. Kat walked over to Nyzir and gave him a smile and a brief hug before turning her attention to the empress. Sylia appraised them calmly before motioning them to follow. They made their way through the back gate of Minraz with little opposition.

They walked across an acre of healthy grass before arriving at the burial site outside of a forest. Nyzir's eyes widened in shock. The coffins of the dead mystics were like nothing he had imagined. Each one was made of the same element that the Mystic wielded in life. The most impressive ones to him were made out of wind and water. Somehow they had been manipulated to stay in a single form, with the bodies inside floating endlessly.

Nyzir had been told that they buried their dead in their element because mystics believed that in the next world, they would still need to protect their kin, and they hoped to bring their power with them. Nyzir glanced around and noticed the amount of dead stretched across the width of the forest where he stood. Seeing the amount of bodies made Nyzir's heart drop into his stomach. They had lost so many. Nyzir had heard at least half of the Forsworn were gone as well as several dozen mystics. As his eyes traveled over the coffins, Nyzir noticed that they were positioned by rank, with apprentices being at the edge and, Nyzir assumed, the captains closer to the center. With that thought, Nyzir moved quickly toward the middle area of forest, scanning each for a familiar name.

He passed a coffin made of compact earth and stopped. Etched into the front was the name Carter, and under it was "Forsworn Captain." A lump formed in Nyzir's throat, and his guts twisted as he stared at the grave that held his dead father. In the deafening silence, he heard soft footsteps. Nyzir turned and saw a large contingent of mystics, Forsworn, and civilians moving toward the burial site.

Kat and Sinera moved to stand with Nyzir as they waited for everyone. Nyzir and Sinera noticed their mother making a beeline for them and grabbing the two in a rough embrace. They hugged her back with as much comfort as they could manage before Helena released her children. Wiping away stray tears, Helena looked at her husband's grave blankly before a slow smile graced her. Bending down, she placed a red lily in front of the coffin.

In a voice barely above a whisper, she spoke. "You gave me this type of flower when you confessed to me. I remember you being nervous. Even when our children were released into this world and you were promoted, I still see that young man standing before me, all flustered." Her grin broadened slightly as she rested a hand on the coffin. "Now it's my turn to give you something for our journey together in the next world." She stood up carefully before stepping back.

Nyzir knelt before the coffin and placed a hand to the soft earth beneath him. He felt the miniscule crystals in the earth claw their way out of the ground and take form. They climbed atop one another and wove around themselves, taking a humanoid appearance. Nyzir focused sharply and commanded the crystals to show more detail. Nyzir felt like he was creating a clay sculpture as he manipulated his power. Before long, he released the crystal and admired his handiwork. Behind the flower his mother had placed stood two figures made out of multicolored gems. The man wore formal cloths of ruby red and bore a smile as he gazed forward. The woman had a dress made of sapphires while she held his arm with her own. To Nyzir's eye, they depicted a loving couple just returning from a dance or wedding. Nyzir gazed at the immortalization of his parents with a proud look before gesturing Sinera and Kat over.

Moving as one, the girls crouched beside Nyzir, with Sinera pulling out her water skin. Nodding to Kat, Sinera poured a generous amount into her cupped palm before turning it to ice with a slow breath. Carefully snapping it in half, Sinera handed Kat a piece and went to work. Sinera molded the ice as she had been trained. Like crystal, ice required a certain analytical mind-set to use. Because of her more impulsive personality, it had proven difficult for her to attain such a state of mind. However, she had found that when she used water, it calmed her mind to allow her to think more clearly.

Sinera eyed the coffin that held her father, and inspiration struck her. She set about modeling her ice after the mace that lay against the coffin. It proved more complicated than she had initially thought, for she sought to create a perfect replica of the weapon, and the detail inlaid in the metal was tricky to copy. She took a slow breath and continued her work. Glancing at Kat, she raised an eyebrow at the fact that Kat was crafting a rose. It looked rough around the edges but still a worthy piece. Sinera smiled as she finished her model before placing it next to Nyzir's piece.

A pleasant chill came over her, and a subtle vibration was felt near her breast. Fishing out the necklace Micenta had given her, she eyed it curiously as it gently pulsed like a miniature heart. Again, she felt that rush of comforting chill. While she may not have understood what the goddess's plans were, she knew this was Micenta showing that she knew what was happening and trying to be there for her even in a small way.

Sinera smiled at the thought and noticed Kat had placed the rose down and was whispering to herself. Sinera made out, "He was a good man, and I'll protect them."

Kat stood, and Sinera followed suit before moving toward Nyzir and Helena. Time seemed to be traveling through honey as the minutes crept by. Nyzir watched as tears were shed among loved ones and friends grieving for the dead. He was shocked when he felt both Sinera and Kat grasp him tightly into a hug. Nyzir could feel them trembling slightly, so he embraced them back. For several minutes, they just held each other for desperate comfort before they were separated by the presence of Sylia. The empress was flanked by two Forsworn, each holding a chest. Sylia stood in front of the gathered mass of people and spoke with a confidence that captivated Nyzir.

"It gives me great pleasure to see you all before me, you brave and wonderful people. As you all know, our home was attacked three days ago by a horde of monsters. If not for the efforts of every mystic and Forsworn, we would have fallen. Know that I am more than grateful to all of you. I'm sure you are all wondering how we were able to repel the dragon and beasts that were clawing at our doorstep. Understand, please, that I cannot explain everything as this knowledge is traditionally only to be known to the current empress and her assigned successor."

Sylia took a deep breath before releasing it slowly. She continued, "The golden dome that protected our city was, in fact, my unique magic. It is the element of light. A rare magic passed down from generations of empresses. Unfortunately, as I'm sure you have noticed, it does take a toll on me when I use it. This is why I only use it when there is no other option."

She seemed to sway slightly with the breeze as she finished before gesturing the Forsworn behind her to her side. When they stood with her, she pressed on.

"Know that I am deeply sorry for those who gave their lives in defense of our home. Many of them were friends of mine and will not be forgotten. We still suffered a heavy loss, which is why we need new mystics in our ranks, and two of them are among us now." Here, her eyes flashed toward Nyzir, Sinera, and Kat. With a smile written on her face, Sylia said, "Nyzir and Sinera, you have proven yourselves both in the defense of our home and with what Sevastian has told me of your training. Open a chest and pick which path you will take."

Nyzir and Sinera approached as the Forsworn lowered the chests. Nyzir opened his, and several items lay bare inside. There was a thin scroll with the mystic insignia tucked into the side of the chest. Nyzir knew it was for those who became mentors. A leather bracer was the second item to draw his eye, inlaid with various intricate designs and appearing sturdy enough to take a light hit. Thinking back to all the Forsworn garbed in their oiled leather made Nyzir understand this was for Forsworn. A neatly folded gray cloak with a narrowed eye lay as a symbol of the scouts. Its eye seemed to follow Nyzir as he examined each item and weighed his decision.

He immediately discarded becoming a mentor as teaching never appealed to him. Becoming a Forsworn would allow him to further honor his dead father and to watch over his home, although he had found that traveling Minraz held a certain appeal to him as well as stopping any threats before they could cause harm. His thoughts turned toward the looming threat of the monsters that roamed the land and the malevolent presence of this dragon on the horizon. Steeling his resolve, Nyzir withdrew the scout cloak and presented it to Sylia. Quickly glancing at his sister, Nyzir saw she had also grabbed the cloak and waited.

Sylia looked at the siblings imperiously before saying with a smile, "If that is your choice, then I pronounce you two to be scouts."

To Nyzir, the sounds of exclamation from the crowd were dimmed to nonexistence by his pounding heart. Warmth swept through him as he felt the Forsworn drape the cloak over his shoulders and fasten it securely. Nyzir rose with his sister in tow, only to be grabbed by Kat and Helena. Found in a four-way hug, with his sister joining in, Nyzir could only smile happily as he embraced them back.

The clearing of a throat was heard, and Nyzir saw Empress Sylia giving them a slightly exasperated look before finding her voice. "I appreciate your enthusiasm, but please allow me to finish before you celebrate as there is one more person I would like to welcome. Kat, please approach."

Kat stiffened slightly before approaching the empress warily. When she stood before Sylia, Kat gave a slight bow of her head before looking the empress in the eye. Sylia purposefully looked all over Kat's body, lingering on the various scars, and then stopped at her face. For several seconds, both women just stared at each other's faces, neither blinking. The only thing that marred Sylia's neutral face was a faint hardening of the eyes and upward curve of her mouth.

Sylia's voice broke the tension like a stone to glass. "I welcome you to our home, Kat, though I wish it were under better circumstances. Sevastian explained to me your part in their training as well as your participation in our home's defense, which I am grateful for."

Sylia grabbed a small pin and presented it to Kat, who examined it with interest. It depicted a bronze star with a small flake of snow at its core. Sylia stepped closer and placed the pin on the front of Kat's animal-hide top before stepping back.

"With this, I name you a friend of Minraz. You will be welcome to stay or come and go as you wish. However, I must know what your intentions are."

Kat appeared calm on the outside, though Nyzir could tell speaking before a crowd was foreign to her if the clenching of her fist and tightening of the jaw attested. "I wanted t' know what the world was like outside my home, which was the main reason I accompanied them. After what I've seen and done with Nyzir, Sinera, and Sevastian, I want to keep them safe and stop this damn dragon!" Kat took a shallow breath. "I know the lot of you are wary of me, being from up north and all, but I ain't gonna just lie down and let some beast stomp me without biting back." Kat flashed a savage grin. "Sevastian let me come along with him, so I've grown attached to him, Nyzir and Sinera. If they care about this place, then it must be worth protecting. Those are my intentions, and know that I'm honored to be a friend of Minraz."

Sylia smiled and squeezed Kat's shoulder before releasing her. Kat moved confidently to stand with Nyzir and Sinera. There was a smattering of applause and cheers from the crowd, and Kat looked at Nyzir with mischievous intent. Using the noise and bodies to her advantage, Kat slipped close to Nyzir and kissed him full on the mouth. Nyzir's eyes widened in shock before they closed slowly.

After a second, Kat broke it and whispered in his ear, "Looks like you're stuck with me, Nyzir."

Nyzir, feeling suddenly bold, replied just as quietly, "I don't think I'll mind that, Kat."

She winked, only to see Sylia looking at her and Nyzir with a sly smile. They both felt heat in their faces as they separated quickly and tried to act casual. Sylia's grin widened slightly before she noticed Sevastian approaching. Glancing subtly at Nyzir and Kat, who were occupied with Sinera and Helena, Sylia felt Sevastian stand next to her and watch the proceedings with an impassive mask.

Deciding to break the ice, Sylia whispered, "Is there no way for me to convince you to abandon your fool's errand?"

Sevastian shrugged. "He will only be a problem in the future. I have to correct what I should have long ago."

Sylia lips tightened. "You are needed here, not traipsing across Thaysia."

"I am doing this with or without your approval. The bastard targeted my apprentices. I'm not going to let him get away with that."

"You always were stubborn. Someday, I predict, it will get you killed. If you are so determined, I feel I should respect your decision as a friend. I wish you safe travels on this hunt."

Sevastian sighed gratefully before glancing at his former students. Seeing them brought a smile to him. "You set me up with them on purpose, didn't you?"

Sylia merely batted an eye. "Now why would I do that, Sevastian?"

Sevastian growled, "Trying to get a straight answer out of you is like trying to tell Nyzir not to do one of his aerial stunts—utterly pointless."

Sylia grinned. "They may be foolish, but you should let him get his thrills as much as he can. With what's to come, I worry about them."

Sevastian appeared slightly hurt. "I trained them with as much time as I was given. Trust me. They're strong enough for this."

Sylia's smile thinned to a narrow line. "Need I remind you that we are threatened by a being that even our founders couldn't fully put down? I know they are skilled. However, that is not all we need to stop this dragon."

Sevastian stayed silent, weighing a response that could maybe lessen his empress's justifiable worry. "I trust them to find a way to pull through. They're more resourceful than you'd think." The words sounded more like self-reassurance, even to him. He bowed slightly to Sylia and then went back to Minraz.

Sylia gazed at Nyzir and Sinera sadly. Their father had vouched for Sevastian when his information was put to scrutiny, so why did she doubt him? Maybe it was the circumstances. Nyzir and Sinera were both very young to be considered mystics. There would be some judgment placed on them by the more experienced mystics. A regretful sigh escaped her. She wished that their training hadn't been so rushed, but the world never did play fair. Steeling herself for her inevitable meetings with the remaining Forsworn captains, Empress Sylia made her way purposefully back to her tower.

Sevastian moved swiftly through Minraz, half-heartedly acknowledging both friends and strangers who recognized him. His mind was going at speeds a hummingbird would be jealous of. He patted a pocket and felt the neatly folded letter inside, though it brought him no comfort. He regretted what he was about to do not just for himself but also for those he cared about.

As he dodged and weaved through the returning people, he finally reached his destination. Steeling himself with an even breath, Sevastian knocked on the plain-looking door. The sound of soft footsteps was heard, and when the door opened, the face of the woman who had stolen his heart stared at him with the warmth of a hearth. Lori ushered him inside and closed the door behind them. Though Sevastian appreciated the privacy, he couldn't help but think he had just caged himself. He shook off the troubling thought in time to reciprocate Lori's enthusiastic greeting. Separating sadly, Sevastian withdrew the letter and placed it in Lori's palm. Looking into her soothing gray eyes made Sevastian's heart ache. Deciding to get to the point, Sevastian spoke.

"Lori, please understand what I'm saying is not just about me but also about you as well as Nyzir and Sinera, and I want you to not interrupt until I finish. Understand?"

Lori looked apprehensive about the discussion but gave her consent with a nod.

Releasing a slow breath, Sevastian continued, "I will be leaving Minraz for a few days, maybe even weeks, to kill my brother."

Lori opened her mouth to speak, but Sevastian's hard gaze stopped her.

"I'm doing this because he has proved himself to be a threat to us. On the way back to Minraz, he attacked me with the hope of killing my apprentices in an effort to hurt me. While he obviously failed, I let him flee. Now I have to put an end to him because if he could find me, then he may be able to locate you. I don't know what would happen if you died or were used as leverage against me."

By now, tears were starting to fall down Sevastian's cheeks. Lori wordlessly embraced him, gripping him tightly. His shaking and sobbing frightened her, for she hadn't seen Sevastian break down like this since his sister's death and brother's desertion. Several minutes passed before Sevastian's sobbing ceased.

Regaining some control over his breathing, Sevastian wiped away the tears before whispering, "I love you. You know that, right? That's why I'm doing this. If you don't hear from me in a week's time, open that letter."

He was surprised when Lori refused to loosen her grip, her knuckles turning white as she spoke. "I know you do, and I understand your reasons, even if I disagree. I can look after myself, Sevastian, or have you forgotten how often I had you on your back during training?"

A light chuckle escaped Sevastian as he retorted, "I seem to recall besting you just as much. Besides, I think you like seeing me on my back."

He grinned as he saw her face flush before she lightly slapped his chest, which caused a chuckle out of them both. Lori loosened her grip, allowing Sevastian to step back before grabbing a sack he had loaded with basic provisions. He gave Lori a quick kiss before he made his way to the door. Lori grasped his arm, forcing him to turn.

"Don't do anything that will make me have to come after you," Lori joked.

Sevastian could tell even though her words held mirth, the gray eyes that locked with his conveyed only concern and worry. Sevastian smiled gently before saying, "You don't have to worry about me. I can look after myself as well."

Lori's eyes softened before she finally let him go. Sevastian moved briskly through Minraz, stopping here and there to greet both friends and strangers. Sevastian examined the damage and reconstruction of his home with sorrow. To his knowledge, many of the buildings had been destroyed, while only a few had escaped unscathed.

When he reached the main gate, he paused as he heard his name being called. Turning, he was greeted with Nyzir, Sinera, and Kat running toward him. Sevastian sighed. His hope of leaving uninterrupted had not been met, though he was secretly glad his former apprentices came to see him off. Nyzir was the first to reach him and paused for a second before eyeing Sevastian.

"Mas—er, Sevastian," Nyzir corrected himself. "Why are you leaving? Surely, you'd be more useful here than leaving."

Kat and Sinera arrived as Nyzir finished and waited for Sevastian's answer. Sevastian sighed, but a smile crept up his face as he moved toward the stables, with Nyzir, Sinera, and Kat following. Sevastian appraised the horses before settling on one with a chestnut coat and white hair surrounding its eyes. After quickly instructing the stable boy on what horse he needed, Sevastian addressed Nyzir's question.

"Surely you, Nyzir, would understand that I don't like to leave things unfinished. I'm off to *correct* a mistake of mine."

Nyzir looked slightly confused. Then his eyes widened, but before he could speak, Sinera interrupted him.

"You're going after Williem, aren't you?"

Sevastian raised an eyebrow at Sinera before nodding.

Kat glared at Sevastian before snapping. "And why are you doing it now when you could've killed him in the forest?"

Sevastian stared at Kat blankly till she averted her gaze. Sevastian spoke calmly to Kat. "The immediate safety of our home was more important than killing a beaten foe. Minraz is at least safe for now. I'm going to stop my brother before he can cause more harm."

Sinera was about say something, but Sevastian held up a hand, and she closed her mouth.

Sevastian grinned. "I know you three can survive without me. You're scouts, after all. Wear that cloak with pride."

The stable boy gave Sevastian the reins before scurrying off.

Sevastian's smile never wavered. "If all goes like I hope, we should meet in a week's time. If something happens, know that it was an honor to have trained you three."

Sevastian got on the horse and gave an encouraging nod to Nyzir and Sinera. He flashed a wink at Kat, which caused her to roll her eyes. Sevastian chuckled wryly before racing out of Minraz.

Nyzir sadly watched him go. Over the months, Sevastian had felt like an elder brother to not just him but Sinera as well. He glanced at his sister to see her holding the necklace she had gotten, her mouth moved silently. Nyzir guessed that Sinera was praying to the supposed ice goddess she had met.

When Sinera finished, Kat spoke. "I know you're worried 'bout Sevastian, but I know it'll take a lot to bring that man down. He'll be fine."

Nyzir felt a little comfort, though he knew Kat was as concerned as he was. He knew he would have to have faith in his former mentor, and with what was going to happen in the next few days, Nyzir would need to be ready. He eyed the empress's tower with reverence. Sylia had always been a beacon to the people of Minraz, and they would need her more than ever.

Adopting a confident smile, Nyzir strode back to his home, with Sinera and Kat keeping him company. He didn't know what would happen, but he did know that he would make his father proud and bear the scout's title with honor.

EPILOGUE

Williem staggered through a canopy of trees, wincing at whatever touched him. His eye scanned the ground and surrounding area for traps or food when a spike of pain forced him to place a hand over his ruined eye. Though he had bound it up with a makeshift bandage, it did nothing for the pain that girl's arrow had caused. Repressing the memory with a growl, he forced himself to keep moving. Squinting at the sun, Williem began moving in what he guessed was the way out.

An hour's travel found Williem on the outskirts of a small village—if you could call several houses and an inn a village. As he debated what to do, he heard footsteps on the rough grass and turned to see three burly men staring him down. Each was armed with a rusted sword, and they wore tattered armor. Williem gave a sigh of contempt. Why did he have to deal with low-life bandits?

One of the bandits spoke in a rough voice. "Oi, hand us your valuables, or you're dead."

His friends gave rough nods and brandished their weapons threateningly.

Williem almost felt pity for these fools, but that was overtaken by a feeling of bloodlust. After his humiliating defeat, he needed to vent, and it seemed Lady Luck smiled at him. Adopting a wolfish grin, Williem drew his sword with a deliberate slowness, eyeing his foe's reactions. The one who'd spoken merely tightened his grip on his sword, while his friends looked shocked that their prey would think of fighting back.

With a cry, the apparent leader lunged at Williem with a rough series of strikes. Williem effortlessly parried and dodged and waited for the other two to join in. He didn't have to wait long as soon, all of them were locked in the jaws of battle. Williem used his speed to the fullest, outmaneuvering their clumsy attacks and setting them up to get in one another's way. Williem ducked a beheading strike and ran his sword through the unfortunate bandit's chest. Without pause, he withdrew the blade with a shower of red before intercepting a strike that would have severed his right leg.

His peripheral vision showed him a blade trying to copy the dead bandit's final move. Williem rolled backward in time to miss the blow and heard a scream of agony. Glancing up, he saw with satisfaction that the leader's blade was lodged in his follower's side and that he was trying to pull it out quickly. Deciding to savor the moment, Williem waited patiently as the leader extracted his sword and left the dying bandit on the ground.

Williem felt playfulness intertwine with his bloodlust as he danced with his enemy. He savored every nick and scratch he inflicted and relished the frustration that showed on the leader as he continually failed to kill him. It continued till Williem began to feel the ice of fatigue set into his bones. Though disappointed he couldn't continue, Williem knew sacrifices had to be made sometimes. Redirecting a chop meant to split his head open, Williem drove his elbow into his opponent's wrist. The bandit's wrist cracked, causing a shout of pain before Williem knocked his legs out, forcing him to the ground. Before the bandit could react, Williem jabbed his blade in between the eyes of the man.

Williem felt the rush of successful battle as he cleaned off his sword. Glancing at the town, he saw that some people were beginning to move about. Guess it was time to greet his new neighbors, but first, he had to dispose of his trash. Planting a hand on the bandit leader's chest, he sent waves of magma across the dead body. The smell of burning flesh and hair made him smile as the body liquefied. He repeated the process on the other two.

Examining the remains, Williem was satisfied that no one would know of his killings, which would only have been an annoyance to explain. He schooled his face and checked his clothes for blood. Seeing none, he set about strolling toward the village, humming as he went.